NEW YORK REVIEW BOOKS

CLASSICS

THE WINE-DARK SEA

LEONARDO SCIASCIA (1921–1989) was born in Racalmuto, Sicily. Starting in the 1950s, he made a name for himself in Italy and abroad as a novelist and essayist, and also as a controversial commentator on political affairs. Among his many other books are *The Day of the Owl*, *Equal Danger*, and *To Each His Own* (also published by New York Review Books), works in a genre that Sciascia could be said to have invented: the metaphysical mystery.

ALBERT MOBILIO is a poet and critic. His books of poetry include *Bendable Siege* and *The Geographics*, and his criticism has appeared in *Harper's*, *The New York Times Book Review*, and *The Village Voice*. In 1999 he won the National Book Critics Circle award for excellence in reviewing.

THE WINE-DARK SEA

Leonardo Sciascia

■

Translated by

AVRIL BARDONI

Inroduction by

ALBERT MOBILIO

NEW YORK REVIEW BOOKS

New York

THIS IS A NEW YORK REVIEW BOOK
PUBLISHED BY THE NEW YORK REVIEW OF BOOKS

Copyright © by the Leonardo Sciascia Estate
Introduction copyright © 2000 by Albert Mobilio
Translation copyright © 1985 by Avril Bardoni
All rights reserved.

Published in Italy as *Il Mare Colore del Vino* by Adelphi Edizioni, Milan

This edition published in 2000 in the United States of America by
The New York Review of Books, 1755 Broadway, New York, NY 10019

Library of Congress Cataloging-in-Publication Data
Sciascia, Leonardo.
  [Mare colore del vino. English]
  The wine-dark sea / Leonardo Sciascia ; translated by Avril Bardoni ;
introduction by Albert Mobilio.
      p. cm.
  ISBN 0-940322-53-6 (acid-free paper)
  I. Bardoni, Avril. II. Title.
  PQ4879.C54 M313 2000
  853'.914—dc21

                              00-010122

ISBN 0-940322-53-6

Book design by Red Canoe, Deer Lodge, Tennessee
Caroline Kavanagh, Deb Koch
Printed in the United States of America on acid-free paper.
10 9 8 7 6 5 4 3 2

November 2000
www.nybooks.com

CONTENTS

INTRODUCTION

LEONARDO SCIASCIA, DESPITE the catchy melody of his name and his several translated books, remains largely unknown in America. Famous in Europe for politically sophisticated detective novels buffed to a high literary gloss, replete with meditations on Mallarmé and "Pirandellian" characters, he never benefited from the vogue for Italian fiction that spotlighted Calvino, Levi, and Eco. Partly to blame may be the decidedly political character of his work. Sciascia began his career in the 1950s when social realism was the order of the day for Italian writers. His first book, *Salt in the Wound*, seemed to fit the bill by providing an acid-edged portrait of life in a Sicilian mining town. But Sciascia proved too cagey for the party line; he snapped sharply at profiteering as well as Leftist orthodoxy. His fondness for the unsettling, enigmatic Sicilian folk tale (a taste he shares with fellow countryman Pirandello) further distanced him from the social-realist goal of political message writ large.

Sciascia's skepticism was hardly unearned. Stints as a Communist Party member of Palermo's town council and as a Radical Party MP in the European Parliament sparked his sly wit. The armchair anarchists, scheming priests, closet mafiosi, and political hacks that people his tales have been lifted whole from the ongoing circus that is Italian and, especially, Sicilian politics. The stories in *The Wine-Dark Sea* delve into this contentious world where church, state, and family make war on each other to ensure that no one comes out ahead. "Privilege, to the Sicilian," Sciascia instructs in one of his early essays, "is not so much the liberty of enjoying certain things as the pleasure of forbidding them to others."

Such vintage malice is on view in "Demotion," a story set in the late 1950s which recounts a crisis of faith for both Catholics and Communists. When the local party boss discovers his wife has joined a prayerful throng at the Cathedral of Saint Filomena he's embarrassed and outraged. Church scholars have announced that the saint never existed, but the town's women pack the pews to halt removal of her statue. The man berates his wife harshly: "She does not exist and she never existed . . . and they will take her down from the altar and put another saint in her place and you will continue to have masses said." Unable to shake her piety, he retreats to his

Communist newspaper only to discover, in small print, shocking news: Stalin's tomb has been moved outside the Kremlin walls. He flings the newspaper aside yet refuses to answer when his wife asks "What's the matter?" A Stalinist Ralph Kramden, he would rather stew in his own bile than allow his wife the smallest satisfaction.

Strategically situated at the crossroads of Europe and Africa, Sicily has been occupied by foreign powers almost continuously for over 2000 years. A succession of Greek, Roman, Spanish, Norman, French, and Arab invaders leaves open the question of what really is a Sicilian. If it isn't a bloodline, perhaps it is a disposition. In *The Italians*, Luigi Barzini writes: "Everywhere in Italy life is more or less slowed down by the exuberant intelligence of the inhabitants, in Sicily it is paralyzed by it."

This sense of life being fought to a standstill, which permeates Sciascia's view of his homeland, is the subject of his retelling of a popular folk tale, "The Ransom." When the famous judge Don Nicola casts an acquisitive eye at Don Raimondo's daughter, Concettina, Raimondo sees an opportunity to free his son-in-law from prison (he killed a peasant with a single kick). The girl recoils from the bargain but her family's expectations prevail—she marries the old judge. Six months later she wakes to find her husband dead beside her; she then returns to her father's house a widow, albeit a very rich one. Another six months pass and she defies her father by eloping with a young man ("Don Raimondo only forgave them on his death-bed").

The economies of love, duty, and betrayal are delicately calibrated to maintain a kind of existential stasis. The judge gets his child-bride but also, perhaps from exertion, finds his death; Don Raimondo sacrifices his daughter to free the husband of his other daughter, then, miraculously Concettina returns, but only to pay him back in full (and punish herself with the loss of her father) by fleeing him for good. In each relationship, the heart is fought to a draw. At the end of the story Sciascia wryly notes how the "Catholic concept of vicarious payment...has become, in Sicily, a cardinal dogma of the agonizing religion of the family. The guilty ransomed by the innocent."

Sciascia's Sicily is a Gothic locale; its lush, sun-worn landscape, rural inhabitants, and subterranean histories make it a world not unlike Faulkner's South. Sicily too is a land of insurrection, tribal fiefdoms, and baroque rites of honor. With their stiff-necked pride in the face of defeat's long shadow, Sciascia's characters are cousins to Faulkner's. Both groups of "Southerners" have been (and still are in Italy) regarded by many "Northerners" with undisguised disdain. Southern Italians and Sicilians are sometimes called "the blacks" of Europe because of their poverty and perceived backwardness. Although Sciascia's loyalties are hardly in doubt, he sketches out the battle lines of this North–South antipathy without indulging in political agitprop. We follow the adventures of Mr. Blaser, a Swiss recruiter for an electrical company, as he travels around Sicily in "The Test." With his hired driver he moves from town to town administering a dexterity test to young women desperately in need of work. Matter-of-fact in his depiction both of the imperious Blaser as well as the alternately suspicious and obsequious locals, Sciascia locates the resolute heart of cultural and economic difference: "They don't seem to see us," says a young man whose girlfriend is leaving for Switzerland. "It makes you feel like a fly in a spider's web." And, Blaser, coming out of the church where he's given the test, "girls swarming out after him," crisply pronounces, "Primitive place."

What a Sicilian might see as primitive in a non-Sicilian is suggested in another story in which a wife, worried about confessing her adultery to her husband, writes a letter to a women's magazine: "Every priest, except one (but he was a northerner) has told me that if my repentance is sincere . . . I must remain silent." Secrecy, for the Sicilian, is the civilized alternative to brutish honesty. Sciascia shows the Mafia's code of silence, *omerta*, to be diffused throughout the society—the mother who refuses to say a word to the carabinieri about the man she knows murdered her son is close kin to this guilty wife. Both dwell in a sub rosa world of the implicit word and the cloaked gesture. It is a world where deception is only frowned upon to the degree it lacks artfulness. "This is a country," declares one of Sciascia's mafiosi, "where the left hand doesn't trust the right even if they belong to the same man."

"The Long Crossing" recounts a deft and hilariously sad betrayal. Beginning on a empty beach, peasants dig their life savings from shoes and shirts. (The cunning ones have borrowed money, certain they will never have to repay.) Signor Melfa collects the cash and assures a safe landing in New Jersey (between 1890 and 1920 one-quarter of Sicily's population left the island). After eleven days below deck, he summons them up: "Have you ever seen a skyline like this in your part of the world?" Peasants who have never left their village all agree. Once ashore, they soon discover the ruse: they've landed at the other end of Sicily. "Silence descended once more," is how Sciascia describes their reaction. This time silence is not meant to deceive or conceal but rather it signals a profound and melancholic resignation, one which allows the world its duplicities but retains the Sicilian's right not to acknowledge he's been duped. Again, spite proves a divine elixir healing all wounds.

The Sicilian language is the only one in Europe that has no future tense. The island's bitter legacy of conquest and revolt seems to have stunted its inhabitants' ability to conceive of a time outside this recurrent cycle. At the source of Sciascia's conflicted love for his compatriots is his acute understanding of their paralysis, this need to find victory in denying triumph to others. A latter-day Voltaire (his novel *Candido* is an homage to a mentor), Sciascia is at heart a cynic, a descendant of an ancient culture who, in his own lifetime, has witnessed his homeland occupied by the Fascists, the Germans, the Americans, and then returned to the Mafia. History has made him a poet of disillusion. But, like a jeweler displaying gems he values precisely for their defects, Sciascia presents his people and their history for our detailed inspection. In *The Wine-Dark Sea* the specimens come unadorned, dug straight from rocky Sicilian turf, and amply reflect the island's soul, a barbed composite of honor and treachery, brutality and wit.

THE
WINE-DARK
SEA

THE RANSOM

"YOUR MAJESTY," SAID Minister of State Sant-angelo, tapping Ferdinand lightly on the shoulder with one finger, "this is Grotte."

The king awoke with a hiccup, tried to focus his watery eyes, still heavy with sleep, upon the minister sitting opposite him and passed the back of his hand over his mouth from which ran a trickle of saliva.

"What's the matter?" he asked.

"This is the town of Grotte, Your Majesty."

Ferdinand peered out of the carriage window at a jumble of gray houses clinging to the side of a hill, roofs sprouting moss and nettles, black-clad women standing in doorways, children with startled, hungry eyes, pigs rooting among piles of rubbish.

He drew back.

"And what is the reason for my being awoken?" he asked the minister. And continued, as if addressing a third person: "Twenty-four hours without a wink of sleep, and as soon as I manage to drop off this idiot has to wake me up with the glad tidings that we are passing through Grotte!"

His underlip, which looked like a cow's kidney, trembled with vexation. He turned again to the window. A few paces from the carriage a group of silent people was forming.

"Grottoes are infested with wolves. Forward!" he shouted to the escort; then slumped back against the cushions, laughing heartily at his own wit. The minister doubled up with mirth.

They pushed on for another two miles, to Racalmuto where they found the balconies hung with silken drapes as if for the festival of Corpus Christi, the civic guard smartly drawn up and a banquet awaiting them in the town hall.

Thus was Grotte ("Le Grotte" in the documents of the time, "Li Grutti" as the people of Racalmuto still call it) deprived of the honor of receiving King Ferdinand.

Exactly one hundred years later, the train carrying Mussolini sped through the station at Grotte past crowds packed so densely on the platform that they almost overflowed onto the line itself; yet few caught even a glimpse of the bronzed, scowling face of the Duce or the sallow, smiling one of his companion, Starace.

Until only a few years ago, these two incidents continued to inspire a good deal of scorn and derision on the part of the inhabitants of Racalmuto at the expense of those of Grotte. And the latter, for their part, possessed a sizable repertoire of *mimi* (comic playlets in mime after the style of Francesco Lanza, the collector and arranger of a series of such pieces and by whom they were christened *mimi*) which burlesqued the defects of the inhabitants of Racalmuto.

When Grotte met Racalmuto on the football field, the recitation of these historical incidents and of the *mimi*, the hurling of insult and invective, continued until five minutes before the whistle—at which point verbal abuse was replaced by physical assault, by punches, kicks and stone-throwing.

In truth, the two towns, although only separated by a couple of miles, were as different as could be. Grotte had a Protestant minority and a Socialist majority, three or four families of Jewish descent and a strong Mafia; it also had bad roads, mean houses and dreary festivals. Racalmuto staged a festival that lasted a whole week and was splendidly colorful and extravagant; the people of Grotte flocked to it in their hundreds; but for the rest of the year the town was tranquil and trouble-free, being electorally divided between two great families, having a handful of Socialists, an army of priests and a Mafia divided against itself.

Relations between the two towns were sweetened

over the years and their rivalries muted not only by the march of progress but also, undoubtedly, by the frequent marriages between Grottesi and Racalmutesi; marriages which, although for the most part painstakingly arranged by intermediaries, were nevertheless usually happy.

One such marriage, which took place a few years before the demise of the Kingdom of the Two Sicilies, has become part of the folklore of both communities, not because of any element of fairy-tale romance, cruel parental opposition or deeds of blood, but only, perhaps, because of the beauty of a young girl, or possibly because the events that occurred in its wake provide such a clear picture of a particular society at a particular time.

The marriage, between Don Luigi M., a well-to-do doctor of Racalmuto, and a daughter of Don Raimondo G., a wealthy landowner of Grotte, had been celebrated with all the pomp expected of two such families and the life of the newlyweds was running smoothly and harmoniously in the splendid house at Racalmuto, with the husband, a full-blooded man of immense stature, full of shy attentions towards his young bride, a mere slip of a girl, when a dreadful accident occurred. In the course of an argument with one of his tenant farmers, Don Luigi lost his temper and lashed out at the man with his boot. This was, of course, an entirely legitimate way for a gentleman to resolve a dispute with a peasant, but in this case either the peasant was not endowed with the same robust constitution as Don Luigi, or maybe the kick damaged some vital organ; anyway the fact remains, according to the descendant of Don Luigi who told me the story, that the man, after staggering three times round the room, fell under a table, curled himself into a ball, and died.

The law was to be reckoned with even in those days; though more timid, more biddable where gentlemen were concerned, a corpse was a corpse and Don Luigi faced inevitable arrest. He fled, leaving his young bride alone in the splendid house.

At the social club there was an immediate sense of outrage among the élite citizenry—not, of course, directed at poor Don Luigi. Old Don Ottavio, in his bitterness of heart, coined a phrase which achieved immediate currency and which has remained in use as an ironic adage to this day: "What a world we live in nowadays, when a gentleman can't even kick a peasant!" Everyone agreed with him: the world was indeed in a sorry state!

Don Luigi had certainly not gone very far; he might even have been in Grotte, staying with relatives or friends he could trust. But it was still inconvenient, and the thought of his young wife, alone and afraid, all frills and tenderness, lying in the big bed with its silken damask hangings, tortured him unbearably.

The good offices of influential friends were sought in an attempt to spirit away the warrant for his arrest: the warrant which, garnished with the delicate butterfly-like emblem of the Bourbon lilies, the Captain of the Guard kept hanging on a nail beside his office desk. Don Luigi's father-in-law, a man of great resource and a vast circle of friends, had tried in vain for some considerable time to discover "the right string to pull" when, by a stroke of sheer good luck, it fell into his hands one December evening when he was sitting in his dressing gown by the fireside, reading *Il Monitore* while his daughter Concettina worked away at her embroidery, in coral beads and gold thread, of a picture of the Infant Jesus totally naked except for a band from which hung, dangling between the crooked baby legs, a little bell. The original from which Concettina was copying was a devotional image given to her by her aunt who was a nun. Don Raimondo considered the little bell to be in grossly bad taste but kept his counsel, fearing to cast doubt both upon the innocence of the nuns, who held the image in veneration, and upon that of his daughter who was copying the picture with such loving attention. But the thought of that little bell gnawed at him as he read his paper and he determined to speak to his wife about it and ask her to persuade Concettina to relinquish the embroidery.

Thus, when his thoughts were interrupted by a furious knocking at the front door, the first words that came to his lips as he went to open it were: "Put that little bell out of sight!" And when Concettina failed to grasp his meaning, he cried: "That thingummybob . . . the Infant Jesus," fearing that the visitor, whoever he was, might make mischief on the subject of Concettina's purity.

The visitor was a personage of some importance, no less than Don Nicola Cirino, jurist and poet, Procurator General of Palermo. His carriage had broken down at the gates of Grotte, in a night of bitter cold and howling wind, and, unable to continue his journey, he had been accompanied to Don Raimondo's house, the best in town.

Don Nicola was a man of about sixty, with gray hair and a gray beard, somewhat wizened and with a general air of decrepitude; but his eyes were piercing and lively, contrasting curiously with the impression of bone-weariness and imminent collapse.

Don Raimondo, whose reactions were always swift, directed a prayer of thanksgiving to the Almighty for having sent a night such as this, positioned a stone on the road and arranged for the coachman to suffer a moment's distraction. For these were the circumstances, as Don Nicola explained while apologizing for the inconvenience to which he was putting the household, which had caused the accident.

Don Raimondo assured him that far from being an inconvenience, this was an honor, a pleasure . . .

Concettina had put away her embroidery. Don Raimondo now presented her to Don Nicola and, in her shyness, she blushed the color of a ripe peach. Her beauty was extraordinary: a graceful figure, hair the color of caramel and a face that combined a timid sweetness with irrepressible gaiety, the gaiety that can see the comic side of everything, including trouble. Don Nicola was moved to thoughts—in verse—of a branch of wild roses, of oranges cradled in green foliage beneath the snow, of the morning star . . . And, still in the poetry which came so easily to him when he was inspired by beauty, he compared his heart to a volcano erupting with molten streams of passion. Since he already knew all about the warrant issued for the arrest of Don Raimondo's son-in-law, all the codices, Pandects, indictments and sentences lay from that moment like votary offerings at the feet of a sixteen-year-old girl.

It was a very pleasant evening. The improvised supper turned out splendidly. Seals bearing the imprint of that unpropitious year 1848 were broken but the wine in their bottles proved to be excellent. On top of that, the imprint of 1848 served as a pretext for the introduction of topics upon which Don Nicola and Don Raimondo held identical opinions. They drank each other's health. Don Nicola proposed toasts in verse to the mistress of the house, who, in her hastily-donned satin, had assumed the splendor of a rose in full bloom, and to Concettina. Then, in response to requests from Don Raimondo, the signora and, shyly, from Concettina, he recited a poem he had written about Torquato Tasso. When he arrived at the lines:

> Tho' darkling pleasures sweetened bitter days
> For that great, grieving soul, yet was his life
> So trammell'd and oppress'd that from his heart
> All hope, alas! had fled, and torment reigned

> To gnaw and burn unceasingly; his sighs
> Were those of one who almost feeds on grief.
> If he might be consoled by loving tears,
> Divine compassion, tenderness of heart,
> Eleonora . . .

he fastened upon Concettina the languishing gaze of a dying man, and, leaning over the table towards her, pronounced the name "Eleonora" in a way that left no doubt but that he meant "Concettina"; this was not lost upon Don Raimondo and his wife, who exchanged worried glances.

After complimenting the poet, Don Raimondo skillfully edged the conversation round to the subject of the misfortune suffered by another daughter of his, whose husband, under threat of arrest, had been forced to flee God knows where, leaving the girl, only a few months after her wedding, all alone; and all because of a peasant having been kicked . . . At this rate, society was in a fair way of being stood on its head . . . Yes, the law had to be obeyed; but one foolish kick in a moment of temper . . .

Don Nicola seemed to have withdrawn into some world of his own; he watched Concettina and said nothing. He was weighing up the pros and cons of a scheme he had in mind; he had already decided to chance his arm, but was still undecided as to whether he should do so at once or wait until morning.

"Can we have a word in private?" he asked suddenly, the decision made.

Mother and daughter arose in some slight confusion, and, at a nod from Don Raimondo, left the room.

Swirling the wine around the bottom of his glass, Don Nicola said with a smile, "Don Raimondo, would you like to have your son-in-law back with you in time for Christmas?"

"Need you ask?" said Don Raimondo, thinking: "With a man in his position, this could cost me a fortune."

Neither spoke for a few moments.

"Contrary to what you're thinking, I'm not talking about money," said Don Nicola, "but about something infinitely more valuable, something which is, to both you and me, not only precious but priceless. Can you not guess?"

"Saint Anthony Abbot!" exclaimed Don Raimondo, who invariably invoked the patron saint of the town in moments of crisis. He had indeed guessed, and the effect was cataclysmic, making, for the moment, all thought impossible.

"I see I have shocked you, and appreciate the reasons for such a reaction. I assure you that a refusal would not surprise me in the least, and should that happen, this sociable evening that we have spent would still remain a very pleasant memory. But I'm sure you understand things; given my position, if I were to do all that I am disposed to do and that is in my power to do, on behalf of a brother-in-law, a relation, no one would offer a word of criticism. People would merely say: 'He saved his brother-in-law from prison, anyone would do the same.' But for a complete stranger . . ."

"You're right," said Don Raimondo.

"I'm glad you understand. So give it some thought, discuss it with your wife, and with your daughter . . . And let me know your decision tomorrow before I leave. And now we won't mention the subject again until tomorrow."

Don Raimondo summoned the maid and sent her to inform the ladies that they might return. His wife searched his face anxiously, trying to read his thoughts. They drank cordial and Concettina played devotional songs and romances at the piano while Don Nicola gazed at her besottedly, leaning so low over the instrument that his head seemed about to drop onto the keyboard and roll into Concettina's lap.

When the clock chimed midnight, Don Nicola, to the great relief of his hosts, finally decided to retire for the night. He wished them all a good night with many a flowery speech and was barely out of the room before the signora turned upon Don Raimondo. "What did he want?" she asked with avid anxiety.

Without satisfying his wife's curiosity, Don Raimondo turned to Concettina and asked her if she loved her sister. Concettina did indeed. More questions and more answers followed, forming a kind of domestic catechism between father and daughter, Concettina never straying once from a purely orthodox line, from what was expected of her and from the principles of self-sacrifice for which her whole upbringing had so rigidly, yet so tenderly, prepared her.

Finally, having assured himself that Concettina was prepared to help her sister no matter what the cost to herself, Don Raimondo told her that Don Luigi's return to his wife, his lands and his patients, and his exculpation in the eyes of the law, all turned upon her marriage to Don Nicola.

Concettina began to laugh, and laugh, and laugh; then the laughter turned into a convulsive, desperate storm of tears. But when her mother, too, began to weep and even Don Raimondo failed to restrain a trembling tear, she calmed down and between the tears said yes, she would marry Don Nicola.

As everyone was impatient that the thing should be done as quickly as possible, Don Nicola because he was consumed with passion, and Don Raimondo and the family because they wanted Don Luigi free at once, the arrangements were pushed ahead with all possible speed. For a week the house was awash with billows of lawn and crisp new linen, with bedcovers of wool and shining silk in every color of the rainbow. The word "bed," constantly recurring in such permutations as "bedcover" and "bed-linen" ("twenty-four sets of bed-linen for the trousseau") became, in Concettina's mind, a single concrete image of almost feverish repugnance. None of this showed in her face, however, bent with such sweetness over the embroidery upon which the Infant Jesus, complete with little bell, continued to take shape. And Don Nicola regarded her ecstatically; for the old goat in love, the little bell range out in celebration of innocence and added a touch, only a touch, of delicious obscenity.

Thus it came about that the literary work of ample bulk and fundamental importance upon which Don Nicola had been engaged, *The Institution of the Monarchy in Sicily*, remained uncompleted. Love for his child-bride distracted the distinguished lawyer-poet and then gently finished him. Concettina awoke one morning about six months after her marriage to find her husband peacefully dead beside her. He had passed away silently during the night like a candle whose flame leaps once before it gutters into darkness.

Concettina returned to her father's house a widow, and extremely rich.

Six months had not yet passed before she eloped one moonlit night, herself as palely beautiful as the moon in her black widow's weeds, with a young man from Racalmuto who, though he had said nothing, had been in love with her since before her marriage. A handsome, elegant young man of good family, but liberal and spendthrift.

Don Raimondo only forgave them on his death-bed.

I was reminded of this story, which had made a great impression upon me as a boy, when I entered the Church of St. Dominic in Palermo where Don Nicola lies buried together with all the other great Sicilians. And I was moved to write it down by one of those unforeseen promptings that can be inspired by a certain sensation, a chance encounter or a passage in a book. I had been rereading Baudelaire and came across these lines: "Mais de toi je n'implore, ange, que tes prières, Ange plein de bonheur, de joie et de lumières!" These words, and the title of the poem in which they occur, "Reversibilité," echo somewhat ironically the Catholic concept of vicarious payment which has become, in Sicily, a cardinal dogma of the agonizing religion of the family. The guilty ransomed by the innocent. In this case a girl from Grotte had paid the ransom for a man from the neighboring and hostile town of Racalmuto.

THE LONG CROSSING

THE NIGHT SEEMED made to order, the darkness so thick that its weight could almost be felt when one moved. And the sound of the sea, like the wild-animal breath of the world itself, frightened them as it gasped and died at their feet.

They were huddled with their cardboard suitcases and their bundles on a stretch of pebbly beach sheltered by hills, between Gela and Licata. They had arrived at dusk, having set out at dawn from their own villages, inland villages far from the sea, clustered on barren stretches of feudal land. For some of them this was their first sight of the sea, and the thought of having to cross the whole of that vast expanse, leaving one deserted beach in Sicily by night and landing on another deserted beach, in America and again by night, filled them with misgivings. But these were the terms to which they had agreed. The man, some sort of traveling salesman to judge from his speech, but with an honest face that made you trust him, had said: "I will take you aboard at night and I will put you off at night, on a beach in New Jersey only a stone's throw from New York. Those of you who have relatives in America can write to them and suggest that they meet you at the station in Trenton twelve days after your departure ... Work it out for yourselves ... Of course, I can't guarantee a precise date ... We may be held up by rough seas or coastguard patrols ... One day more or less won't make any difference: the important thing is to get to America."

To get to America was certainly the important thing; how and when were minor details. If the letters they sent to their relatives arrived, despite the ink-blotched, mis-spelled addresses scrawled so laboriously on the envelopes, then they would arrive, too. The old saying, "With a tongue in your head you can travel the world," was right. And travel they would, over that great dark ocean to the land of the *stori* (stores) and the *farme* (farms), to the loving brothers, sisters, uncles, aunts, nephews, nieces, cousins, to the opulent, warm, spacious houses, to the motor cars as big as houses, to America.

It was costing them two hundred and fifty thousand lira each, half on departure and the balance on arrival. They kept the money strapped to their bodies under their shirts like a priest's scapular. They had sold all their saleable possessions in order to scrape the sum together: the squat house, the mule, the ass, the year's store of provender, the chest of drawers, the counterpanes. The cunning ones among them had borrowed from the money-lenders with the secret intention of defrauding them, just this once, in return for the hardship they had been made to endure over the years by the usurers' greed, and drew immense satisfaction from imagining the expression on their faces when they heard the news. "Come and see me in America, bloodsucker: I just may return your money—without interest—if you manage to find me." Their dreams of America were awash with dollars. They would no longer keep their money in battered wallets or hidden under their shirts; it would be casually stuffed into trouser pockets to be drawn out in fistfuls as they had seen their relatives do; relatives who had left home as pitiable, half-starved creatures, shriveled by the sun, to return after twenty or thirty years—for a brief holiday—with round, rosy faces that contrasted handsomely with their white hair.

Eleven o'clock came. Someone switched on an electric torch, the signal to those aboard the steamship to come and collect them. When the torch was switched off again, the darkness seemed thicker and more frightening than ever. But only a few minutes later, the obsessively regular breathing of the sea was overlaid with a more human, more domestic sound, almost like buckets being rhythmically filled and emptied. Next came a low murmur of voices, then, before they realized that the boat had touched the shore, the man they knew as Signor

Melfa, the organizer of their journey, was standing in front of them.

"Are we all here?" asked Signor Melfa. He counted them by the light of a torch. There were two missing. "They may have changed their minds, or they may be arriving late . . . Either way, it's their tough luck. Should we risk our necks by waiting for them?"

They were all agreed that this was unnecessary.

"If anyone's not got his money ready," warned Signor Melfa, "he'd better skip out now and go back home. He'd be making a big mistake if he thought he could spring that one on me when we're aboard; God's truth, I'd put the whole lot of you ashore again. And, as it's hardly fair that everyone should suffer for the sake of one man, the guilty party would get what's coming to him from me and from all of us; he'd be taught a lesson that he'd remember for the rest of his life—if he's that lucky."

They all assured him, with the most solemn oaths, that they had their money ready, down to the last lira.

"All aboard," said Signor Melfa. Immediately each individual became a shapeless mass, a heaving cluster of baggage.

"Jesus Christ! Have you brought the whole house with you?" A torrent of oaths poured out, only ceasing when the entire load, men and baggage, was piled on board— a task accomplished not without considerable risk to life and property. And for Melfa the only difference be- tween the man and the bundle lay in the fact that the man carried on his person the two hundred and fifty thousand lira, sewn into his jacket or strapped to his chest. He knew these men well, did Signor Melfa, these insignificant peasants with their rustic mentality.

The voyage took less time than they expected, lasting eleven nights including that of the departure. They counted the nights rather than the days because it was at night that they suffered so appallingly in the overcrowded, suffocating quarters. The stench of fish, diesel oil and vomit enveloped them as if they had been immersed in a tub of hot, liquid black tar. At dawn they streamed up on deck, exhausted, hungry for light and air. But if their image of the sea had been a vast expanse of green corn rippling in the wind, the reality terrified them: their stomachs heaved and their eyes watered and smarted if they so much as tried to look at it.

But on the eleventh night they were summoned on deck by Signor Melfa. At first they had the impression that dense constellations had descended like flocks onto the sea; then it dawned upon them that these were in fact towns, the towns of America, the land of plenty, shining like jewels in the night. And the night itself was of an enchanting beauty, clear and sweet, with a crescent moon slipping through transparent wisps of cloud and a breeze that was elixir to the lungs.

"That is America," said Signor Melfa.

"Are you sure it isn't some other place?" asked a man who, throughout the voyage, had been musing over the fact that there were neither roads nor even tracks across the sea, and that it was left to the Almighty to steer a ship without error between sky and water to its destination.

Signor Melfa gave the man a pitying look before turning to the others. "Have you ever," he asked, "seen a skyline like this in your part of the world? Can't you feel that the air is different? Can't you see the brilliance of these cities?"

They all agreed with him and shot looks full of pity and scorn at their companion for having ventured such a stupid question.

"Time to settle up," said Signor Melfa.

Fumbling beneath their shirts, they pulled out the money.

"Get your things together," ordered Signor Melfa when he had put the money away.

This took only a few minutes. The provisions that, by agreement, they had brought with them, were all eaten and all that they now had left were a few items of clothing and the presents intended for their relatives in America: a few rounds of goat-cheese, a few bottles of well-aged wine, some embroidered table-centers and antimacassars. They climbed down merrily into the boat, laughing and humming snatches of song. One man even began to sing at the top of his voice as soon as the boat began to move off.

"Don't you ever understand a word I say?" asked Melfa angrily. "Do you want to see me arrested? . . . As soon as I've left you on the shore you can run up to the first copper you see and ask to be repatriated on the spot; I don't give a damn: everyone's free to bump himself off any way he likes . . . But I've kept my side of the bargain; I said I'd dump you in America, and there it is in front of you . . . But give me time to get back on board, for Crissake!"

They gave him time and enough to spare, for they remained sitting on the cool sand, not knowing what to do next, both blessing and cursing the night whose darkness provided a welcome mantle while they remained huddled on the shore, but seemed so full of menace when they thought of venturing further afield.

Signor Melfa had advised them to disperse, but no one liked the idea of separation from the others. They had no idea how far they were from Trenton nor how long it would take them to reach it.

They heard a distant sound of singing, very far away and unreal. "It could almost be one of our own carters," they thought, and mused upon the way that men the world over expressed the same longings and the same griefs in their songs. But they were in America now, and the lights that twinkled beyond the immediate horizon of sand-dunes and trees were the lights of American cities.

Two of them decided to reconnoiter. They walked in the direction of the nearest town whose lights they could see reflected in the sky. Almost immediately they came to a road. They remarked that it had a good surface, well maintained, so different from the roads back home, but to tell the truth they found it neither as wide nor as straight as they had expected. In order to avoid being seen, they walked beside the road, a few yards away from it, keeping in the trees.

A car passed them. One of them said: "That looked just like a Fiat 600." Another passed that looked like a Fiat 1100, and yet another. "They use our cars for fun, they buy them for their kids like we buy bicycles for ours." Two motorcycles passed with a deafening roar. Police, without a doubt. The two congratulated themselves on having taken the precaution of staying clear of the road.

At last they came to a roadsign. Having checked carefully in both directions, they emerged to read the lettering: SANTA CROCE CAMARINA—SCOGLITTI.

"Santa Croce Camarina . . . I seem to have heard that name before."

"Right; and I've heard of Scoglitti, too."

"Perhaps one of my family used to live there, it might have been my uncle before he moved to Philadelphia. I seem to remember that he spent some time in another town before going to Philadelphia."

"My brother, too, lived in some other place before he settled in Brooklyn . . . I can't remember exactly what it was called. And, of course, although we may read the name as Santa Croce Camarina or Scoglitti, we don't know how the Americans read it, because they always pronounce words in a different way from how they're spelled."

"You're right; that's why Italian's so easy, you read it exactly how it's written . . . But we can't stay here all night, we'll have to take a chance . . . I shall stop the next car that comes along; all I've got to say is 'Trenton?' . . . The people are more polite here . . . Even if we don't understand what they say, they'll point or make some kind of sign and at least we'll know in what direction we have to go to find this blasted Trenton."

The Fiat 500 came round the bend in the road about twenty yards from where they stood, the driver braking when he saw them with their hands out to stop him. He drew up with an imprecation. There was little danger of a hold-up, he knew, because this was one of the quietest parts of the country, so, expecting to be asked for a lift, he opened the passenger door.

"Trenton?" the man asked.

"*Che?*" said the driver.

"Trenton?"

"*Che trenton della madonna,*" the driver exclaimed, cursing.

The two men looked at each other, seeking the answer to the same unspoken question: Seeing that he speaks Italian, wouldn't it be best to tell him the whole story?

The driver slammed the car door and began to draw away. As he put his foot on the accelerator he shouted at the two men who were standing like statues: "*Ubriaconi, cornuti ubriaconi, cornuti e figli di . . ."* The last words were drowned by the noise of the engine.

Silence descended once more.

After a moment or two, the man to whom the name of Santa Croce had seemed familiar, said: "I've just remembered something. One year when the crops failed around our parts, my father went to Santa Croce Camarina to work during the harvest."

As if they had had a rug jerked out from beneath their feet, they collapsed onto the grass beside the ditch. There was, after all, no need to hurry back to the others with the news that they had landed in Sicily.

THE WINE-DARK SEA

THE TRAIN THAT leaves Rome throughout the summer at 20:50—*"diretto per Reggio Calabria e Sicilia,"* announces a female voice over the loudspeakers, evoking for the stream of passengers making for the train clutching hold-alls and suitcases tied up with string, a vision of the face of a woman just past the first flush of youth floating in the evening sky among the overhead lines of the Termini station—boasts a single first-class carriage Rome–Agrigento, an enormous privilege granted at the request of three or four Deputies from western Sicily who ensure its perpetuation. Actually, of all the through trains to the south, this is the least crowded. In second class it is rare not to be able to find a seat, while in first class, especially in the Agrigento carriage, it is quite possible, by simply turning off the lights, drawing the curtains and distributing one's luggage around the seats, to have a compartment all to oneself at least as far as Naples, and, with a degree of circumspection, all the way to Salerno. After Salerno you can prepare to sleep in comfort, in a singlet perhaps or even going the whole hog and donning pajamas, for no one will enter your particular compartment in search of a seat. Such convenience as regards the seating has to be weighed, however, against the inconvenience of the relative slowness of the journey compared to the express, which leaves two hours earlier and arrives at Agrigento, the end of the line, with at least a seven-hour advantage over the through train. For this reason, most Sicilians opt for the express.

But when Bianchi, a civil engineer traveling to Sicily for the first time—to Gela, to be precise, and on business —found that he would have to travel by rail as all the flights were booked up, he was advised to take the *diretto*, to travel in the Rome–Agrigento carriage and to make a reservation or he might have to stand for a whole night in the corridor. This was bad advice from first to last, particularly concerning the reservation, since in a reserved compartment there are invariably as many travelers as there are seats while in an unreserved one you may well have the whole compartment to yourself. Thanks to this advice, Bianchi inevitably found himself committed to an uncomfortable journey, sharing a compartment with five other people, three adults and two children. The adults were extremely talkative, the children—both boys—lively and undisciplined.

Of the three adults, two were the parents of the unruly children; the third, attached to the family by ties of family, friendship or casual acquaintance, was a girl of about twenty-three, rather colorless at first sight and clad in a severely simple dress of black edged with white. The children never left her alone, the elder boy leaning against her as if he was too sleepy to move, his younger brother repeatedly scrambling up to put his arms round her neck and pull her hair and then scrambling down again to sit on the floor. The bigger one was called Lulu, the smaller one Nene—diminutives, Bianchi learned shortly before the train reached Formia, for Luigi and Emanuele. But before they reached Formia, he knew practically everything about the four members of the family and the girl traveling with them. They came from Nisima in the province of Agrigento, a large rural community with plenty of land and wealthy proprietors; the air was fresh; the local government was social-communist; it was the home town of a notable member of the fascist regime; it had no railway station; it did have an ancient castle. Husband and wife both taught at the elementary school, as did the girl too, though not yet as a permanent member of staff. The family had come to Rome to attend the wedding of the signora's brother (Ministry of Defense, Group A; a power to be reckoned with in the Pensions

Department) to a girl from Rome, a nice girl from a very good family (father in the Ministry of Education, Group A); the bride had a degree in literature and taught in a private school; a lovely girl, tall, fair-haired. They had been married that very day, in the church of San Lorenzo in Lucina, a beautiful church, not to be compared with the church of Sant'Ignazio, but very nice. Witnesses from Group A. The girl, entrusted to their care on the return journey by her brother (in the Ministry of Justice, Group A), had however been holidaying in Rome; she had just recovered from a serious illness and was wearing the black dress edged with white in fulfillment of a vow made to San Calogero, patron saint of Nisima and author of many miracles. The signora wondered why, in the whole of Rome, a city of churches, not one single church was dedicated to San Calogero. "It doesn't seem possible," she said. "Not one church, not even an altar. And he was a great saint."

At the mention of San Calogero the husband gave a small, skeptical smile. The girl confided that, as a child, she had been afraid of San Calogero with his black face, black beard and black cape, and that it had been her mother, rather than she herself, who had made the vow; not that that made any difference: for yet another month (and this was already the sixth) she was committed to wearing the black dress edged with white.

"At the height of summer, with the sun melting the very stones," said the husband.

"That's what a vow's all about," said his wife with a touch of asperity. "A vow that involves no discomfort is no vow at all."

"Isn't it enough that everyone in Rome was turning round to stare at me?" asked the girl.

"No, that's not enough. Mortification and suffering; it takes both to release oneself from such an obligation."

A flicker of scorn showed in the girl's face. Bianchi suddenly saw her in quite a different light. Beneath the drab dress she had beautiful breasts and a shapely body. And her eyes were large and luminous.

"I'm releasing my feet," said the younger child, undoing his shoes and kicking. One shoe stayed on his foot, the other hit Bianchi on the chest.

"Nene!" shouted the parents in tones of warning and reproof. They apologized to Bianchi who, returning the shoe, said, "Nothing to worry about: children will be children . . ." It was, indeed, nothing to worry about compared to what was in store for the unsuspecting Bianchi from the combined efforts of Nene and Lulu during the long journey, particularly when they really got into their stride between Naples and Canicattì.

"All this nonsense about vows!" exclaimed the husband, reviving the subject while replacing his son's shoe. "Antiquated rubbish stemming from ignorance and superstition . . ."

"But you took the *Scala Santa* seriously enough," retorted his wife sharply.

"What has that got to do with it?" said the man, parrying a blow that had evidently found its mark.

"Everything. Let's ask this gentleman what he thinks about that," pursued the woman relentlessly. Bianchi attempted, with a faint smile and a timid hand-gesture, to indicate his unwillingness to be drawn into the argument.

"Oh but you must," said the woman. "You must tell him whether he's consistent or not when he observes all the ritual of the *Scala Santa* and then ridicules vows made to the saints."

"Please do," urged the man, hoping against hope for moral support.

"What is this ritual of the *Scala Santa*?" Bianchi asked, playing for time.

"Don't you know?" marveled the woman.

"I've got a vague idea, but I can't remember precisely . . ." said Bianchi.

"A vague idea, you can't remember . . . Forgive me, but are you a Catholic or not?"

"Why yes, I'm a Catholic, but . . ."

"He thinks the same as I do," broke in the husband triumphantly.

"You went up the *Scala Santa*," his wife repeated, crushing him yet again.

"Only to keep you company," ventured the man.

"I want something to eat!" shouted Nene. "I want some mortadella, I want a banana."

"And I want an orange squash," said Lulu.

"You're not having any mortadella; it brings you out in a rash," said his mother, pointing to some little red spots on Nene's arm.

"Mortadella, or I'll do the same as Don Pietro's donkey," said Nene, with an expression that promised the immediate translation of words into action.

"What does Don Pietro's donkey do?" asked the girl, amused because she obviously knew already.

Nene slid off his seat to give a practical demonstration.

"For heaven's sake!" cried his parents, grabbing hold of him. They explained to Bianchi that Don Pietro's donkey had a habit of lying on his back and waving all four feet furiously in the air. Nene was capable of giving a perfect imitation.

They gave him some mortadella.

"Orange squash," whined Lulu, "orange squash, orange squash . . ."

Everyone, including Bianchi, promised him orange squash when they got to Naples. To get what he wanted, Lulu's policy was to whine while Nene's was to use threats and blackmail. Bianchi preferred Nene's direct, no-nonsense approach: Lulu's whining grated unbearably on his nerves.

Kissed and cuddled by his parents, Lulu quietened down. The interlude had been providential: the tricky subject of the *Scala Santa* had been dropped.

"I see you're not married," the woman declared after a rapid glance at Bianchi's left hand.

"People with a head on their shoulders stay single," joked her husband.

"True, seeing that you did the opposite," she retorted.

"On the contrary," said Bianchi, "I think that people with a head on their shoulders tend to get married sooner or later. With me it will be later rather than sooner, but I shall marry."

"You see?" said the woman reprovingly to her husband. "There speaks a person with sense."

"I was only teasing . . . Seriously, however, speaking generally and objectively, I would say that marriage is a mistake. Speaking for myself, personally I have no reason to regret it. My wife (and I'm not saying this merely because she is present, I really mean it) is an angel . . ."—here his wife lowered her head to conceal the sudden flush of pleasure—". . . and then there are these two little cherubs . . ." He stroked Nene's head, just beside him, and the child responded by rubbing his face, shiny with grease from the mortadella, all over the front of the raw silk dress shirt that his father had had no time to change since his brother-in-law's wedding.

"Your shirt!" cried the woman. Too late: the shirt was now patterned with greasy hieroglyphics.

"My pet," said the father, "you have ruined Papa's shirt."

"I want some more mortadella," said Nene.

"Mention mortadella once more, and the marshal of the carabinieri will come and arrest you," threatened his father.

34

"I won't mention it; I'll eat it," said Nene, skirting skillfully round the veto.

"He's as sharp as a razor," said his father proudly.

"I want some," persisted Nene.

"No, no and again no," said his father.

"As soon as we get home," said Nene, "I shall tell Aunt Teresina that you were saying nasty things about her to Uncle Toto."

"Did we say anything nasty about her?" said his mother, placing her hand on her heart and looking anxious.

"You and Papa. You were telling Uncle Toto that she's stingy, that she never washes, that she's spiteful . . ." The child's memory was formidable.

"I'll give him the mortadella," said his father.

"By all means," agreed his mother, "and when he comes out in a prickly rash all over, he can go and get Aunt Teresina to scratch it for him."

"I shall scratch myself against the wall," said Nene, snatching the mortadella triumphantly from his father.

During the apprehensive silence that now descended like a pall upon Nene's parents, Bianchi's imagination conjured up a picture of Aunt Teresina's face, sharp and shifty-eyed like a ferret. Finally, in order to ease the tension, he announced, "Here we are in Naples already." The lights of the city twinkled through the dark.

His words roused Lulu who had been leaning listlessly against the girl, half asleep. He renewed his demand for orange squash.

As the train drew alongside the platform, Nene's curiosity was roused by the vendors' cries of "*Sfogliate, sfogliate!*" His father explained that *sfogliate* were sweetmeats made from puff pastry with a creamy filling and Nene, with enthusiasm and his habitual courtesy, demanded one. Bianchi treated Lulu to his orange squash and Nene to a *sfogliata*. Such generosity towards the children prompted a flood of gratitude from the parents and formal introductions: *professor* Miccichè, *ingeniere* Bianchi.

Nene, who had registered unutterable disgust at the first bite, now hurled his pastry away, much as one might hurl a bottle of champagne against the hull of a ship being launched, evidently aiming for his father's head and only just missing.

"You gutter-snipe!" cried his parents in unison.

"It's revolting," said Nene. "I want a *cannolo*."

"A *cannolo*?" said his father. "And where do you suppose I can find a *cannolo* here in Naples station?"

"I don't give a shit. I want a *cannolo*," said Nene, revealing a proclivity for strong language unsuspected, until that moment, by the engineer.

The girl laughed. Miccichè and his wife were at their wits' end. They threatened the immediate arrival of the marshal with whip and chain and asked Bianchi to look out into the corridor to see if he was there, for, they said, Nene's lurid language would have summoned him without a doubt. Bianchi looked along the corridor and confirmed that he was indeed on his way.

"The marshal's a shit-head," muttered Nene, frightened but determined not to be cowed.

Husband and wife began to argue about where and from whom Nene had picked up his dreadful expressions. The club to which her husband took the boy every afternoon was, according to the mother, a positive den of foul language; and two men in particular, Calogero Mancuso and Luigi Finisterra, were directly responsible for the deterioration in Nene's language, being youths who had nothing better to do than amuse themselves by corrupting a child. "You can't imagine," she said, turning to Bianchi, "the things they teach him: dreadful things, even about the saints, even about the Pope himself. Luckily they go in one ear and out the other."

Nene's refutation was immediate—"The Pope's a . . ."—but two hands, one of his mother's and one of his father's, shot out and clamped themselves firmly over his mouth, from which the scandalous definition, like water from a burst pipe roughly repaired, still trickled with a degree of audibility.

"You see?" said the signora to Bianchi. "And I thought he had forgotten. That's the kind of thing they teach him."

Of course, this would never have happened, according to the mother, if her husband had been paying attention to the child instead of being totally engrossed in his game of cards. Miccichè had a passion for *quarantotto*.

But according to the father, the truth of the matter was quite different: it was not at the club, forum of elevated sentiments and chaste language, that Nene picked up his colorful expressions, but from the vulgar people who inhabited the courtyard below a balcony of their house, and the blame lay entirely with his wife for allowing the child to remain on this balcony for hours together.

Nene terminated the discussion succinctly: "At the club." Miccichè slumped, utterly confounded, but his wife, instead of gloating, changed the subject as the train drew out of Naples, recalling that they had come to the city on the second stage of their honeymoon, after Taormina.

It was now past midnight. Bianchi thought, "There'll be no sleep here tonight," and toyed with the idea of changing compartments; there were some, indeed, that were almost empty. But he was not actually sleepy, and the irritation that he had felt initially at finding himself burdened with such irrepressibly loquacious company— including those two exasperating children—had been succeeded first by amusement, and now, just as he was on the point of deciding to quit the compartment, by a vague emotion that was not truly affection but indeed rather like it. He had never had much to do with children and had always believed that he would dislike their company; he had always taken care, when traveling, to select a compartment where there were no children; yet Nene decidedly appealed to him. The girl appealed to him too, her every movement, her every word, making her seem more lively, more desirable. "The fact is," he mused, "that a journey is like a representation of life, a synthesis of all its elements, contracted in space and time; rather like a play, indeed; and it re-creates, with a wealth of hidden artifice, all those elements, those influences and relationships which constitute our existence." He decided to tell Miccichè that he was thinking of changing compartments. They would be able to relax more, he said, and the children would have a bit more space.

"I won't hear of it," said the teacher. "You must certainly not put yourself to any such inconvenience on our behalf. If anyone is to move, it should be us."

There was an exchange of compliments and courtesies and the eventual decision was that none of them should move.

Lulù announced that he was sleepy; he wanted the lights turned out.

"I don't want it dark: I've got to see that the marshal doesn't get me," said Nenè, whose conscience was not entirely easy with regard to this officer of the law.

"Turn off the lights!" screamed Lulù. "I want to go to sleep."

Nenè had immediate recourse to means that the marshal himself might have called "physical persuasion": sliding from his seat, he launched himself upon his brother, and bit him in the leg. Lulù yelled and grabbed furiously at his brother's hair. The boys were separated by pinching Nenè's nose to force him to open his teeth and prising open Lulù's fingers one by one. Nenè received a light slap from his father and Lulù a mild scolding.

39

"Tell me, who is this marshal?" Bianchi asked Lulu with a smile.

"He's a shi . . ." Another rapid clamping of hands over Nene's mouth, again not entirely effective.

"You've made Baby Jesus cry. Every time you say naughty things, he cries," said the mother.

"Where is Baby Jesus?" asked Nene.

"He's in heaven and here on earth too. He's everywhere."

"I've never seen him," said Nene frostily.

"You can't see him, but he's here all the same."

"If I can't see him he isn't here."

"Heathen!" said his mother.

"You'll go to hell," commented Lulu.

"Marshals go to hell," said Nene.

Everyone, including his mother, laughed.

"What a wicked little rascal you are!" said his father tenderly, caressing the child. He turned to Bianchi. "Did you hear what he said? Have you ever known another child like him?" His eyes shone with pride.

Bianchi said "Never"—and it was true.

"He's not a bad boy," said the mother, "only highly-strung. And he's amazingly generous: as soon as he has something new, like a toy or a picture-book, he wants to give it away. He would give the house and everything in it to a needy person; the very sight of someone begging sends him completely mad: 'Mama, let's give him a coat, a mattress, some plates . . .' He's convinced that poverty means not having plates and mattresses, and he's obsessed with the idea that beggars sleep on the floor and eat out of the cans that we throw away..."

"They sleep in front of the church," said Nene, "and eat out of tomato tins. I've seen them. And they die."

"Of course they don't die," said his father.

"They do die," said Nene flatly. Then he added: "But I'm going to be a beggar when I grow up, and then they won't die anymore."

"He wants to be a beggar!" scoffed Lulu. "Idiot, I've told you a thousand times: people can be priests, or doctors when they grow up, but not beggars."

"Is it true that you can't become a beggar?" Nene asked his father.

"Of course you can. Why ever not?" Miccichè replied hastily.

"See?" said Nene to Lulu. "You're the idiot: you didn't know that."

"And I shall be a marshal," said Lulu, "so that I can arrest you and all the other beggars."

The blow was a severe one. Nene began to move.

"He's going to bite me!" yelled Lulu, raising his feet ready to repel an attack.

"I'm not going to bite you. I got up because I wanted to stretch my legs. Must I sit down the whole time?" said Nene in tones which oozed hypocrisy, as he sought the approval of the others. But a moment later he sat down again and became lost, to all appearances, in some melancholy reverie. Gradually, sleep over-took him.

The light was turned out, the windows lowered a few inches and the curtains closed. "Let's hope that we can catch a little sleep," said Miccichè, "we've still got an-other fifteen hours' journey ahead. Good night." They all said "Good night," including Lulu who was already more asleep than awake. It was two o'clock.

Bianchi had the girl next to him; Lulu sat next to her on the other side. On the opposite side, Miccichè and his wife sat with Nene between them. Nene slept restlessly, troubled, perhaps, by the arrival on some dream-doorstep of the marshal, cracking his rawhide whip and rattling his handcuffs. One could not say that he was a beautiful child—Lulu was undoubtedly the better-looking—but he had an exceptional quality that opened up a dimension of thought, of feeling, of attachment that Bianchi had never before considered. As he watched the boy, he was con-scious of an emotion that was almost overwhelming: here, it seemed, was an aspect of the meaning of life that had previously escaped him. The significance of his own life, even of his work as an engineer, above all his work as an engineer, consisted definitively in the fact that Nene had lived four years to his own thirty-eight. "One can have no faith in technology without faith in life: it would be futile to put satellites into orbit were it not for the existence of children of four, of children now being born, of children still to be born. Yet our society has begun to see children as a problem, as they already do in America where so much research in pedagogy and medicine is directed at the question of their freedom . . . The point is that children are not a problem. Any society that views them as a problem separates itself from them, provokes a crisis of continuity. Lulu and Nene are not problems for Miccichè and his wife, though they, as teachers, must have had to trot out all those American and Swiss theories for the benefit of the selection board . . . Apropos of the Swiss; that society of theirs, seemingly disinfected of all the germs of tragedy and history, has yet given rise to Max Frisch's Faber. Greek tragedy and the Zurich School of Engineering. And the bombshell bursts in the ancient land of Greece where fate is still alive and waiting, in ambush . . . Wait a moment: I was thinking about children; Faber doesn't come into that . . . Yes he does, but I'm not thinking lucidly enough to deal with it, I'm too sleepy . . . Ah yes, Greece, Sicily: perhaps there's a connection there . . . Classical education, ancient Greece popping up all the time . . . Yes, it's a fact that in Switzerland you only have to look at a child to see exactly what he will be like as an adult Swiss, while in Greece he is an individual, a man . . . And in Sicily too, I would think. These two children . . . Not much discipline in these places: no rules laid down, no techniques, no tradition of instilling discipline; only the bonds of affection; and both the Greeks and the Sicilians believe that there is no problem that cannot be solved by an appeal to the affections . . . Even the problem of death . . ." Waves of sleep washed gently over his mind.

He was woken by the heat. As she slept, the girl's head had fallen onto his chest; she slept deeply, hardly even breathing. A feeling of tenderness and inexplicable joy flooded through the engineer as he became conscious of the hair that nearly brushed his lips, the breast that pressed against the back of his hand. His body, which had been totally relaxed in sleep, now tensed.

All the others were asleep, Miccichè was snoring. They were now traveling through Calabria; every time the train stopped at a station snatches of dialect were audible in the sudden silence. One station was close to the sea and the sound of the water conjured up visions of human faces that came and went like faces in a film, "faded" in and out upon the ebb and flow of the waves. Bianchi felt that he, too, was being penetrated and dissolved: he was experiencing, without consciously realizing it, a profound oneness with nature, with love.

As the train moved off again, Bianchi heard Lulu stir; a few moments later he suddenly found the boy standing in front of him, regarding him with silent amazement and reproof. The child took the girl's face between his hands and, with a great effort, placed her head upright against the headrest. "He's jealous," thought the engineer. "He's jealous because his attachment to the girl is like that of a lover; that's why he has been sitting so quietly, content to be beside her." The girl awoke and realized what had happened. "Forgive me," she said to Bianchi, and then, to Lulu: "Go back to sleep, pet, it's still dark; look, you can have my seat too, then you can stretch out and sleep comfortably."

She settled him down in the larger space and stroked his head. Lulu said nothing; he regarded her with a mixture of resentment and pleading, racked, perhaps, by a pain to which he could give no name. The girl went out into the corridor.

Bianchi waited until Lulu was asleep before he followed her. She was standing at the end of the corridor with her cheek pressed against the window looking as if she were still lost in the world of dreams. Walking towards her, Bianchi said, "He's gone back to sleep," and then, after a long pause, "He's jealous."

"He is fond of me," said the girl.

"He's very different from Nene: more reserved, more sensitive . . Nene is an extraordinary child," said the engineer.

"Nene's a holy terror. You haven't seen the half of it yet . . . He drives poor Lucia absolutely out of her wits."

"Lucia? Is that the signora's name? I thought her husband called her something different."

"He calls her Etta, short for Lucietta . . . My name is Gerlanda, but everyone calls me Dina, short for Gerlandina . . . No one in Sicily is ever called by their real name even if it's a pretty one."

"Gerlanda is a very pretty name."

"I don't like it, the sound's too heavy."

"I've never heard it anywhere else in Italy."

"It's only found in the province of Agrigento: San Gerlando is the patron saint of the city, its first bishop."

"Was San Calogero also a bishop?"

"No, San Calogero was a hermit. There were seven brothers, according to the legend, all called Calogero: one lived in the area of Nisima. Seven handsome old men . . . Calogero means 'handsome old man' in Greek. I don't know any Greek; do you?"

"I've studied it, but I couldn't claim to know much of it."

"I should have liked to study, but my parents said that going to the *liceo* meant I would have to go on to university; and how, they asked, could one possibly let a girl go alone to a city like Palermo?"

"Are Sicilian families all like that?"

"Oh no, not all of them."

"Is your family especially strict?"

"Not really: there are still a lot of people in Sicily who have a certain attitude towards life; they're suspicious . . ."

"What about?"

"They don't trust people in general, or themselves . . . And they're not entirely wrong . . . Before my illness I was less tolerant, more impatient. I wanted to apply for a post on the mainland, to get away . . . I see things differently now: life seems to have become more superficial, everyone seems prepared to cheat everyone else, without exception . . . I'm afraid I'm not explaining myself very well . . ."

"You explain yourself very well indeed."

"When I was sitting in a café in Rome or Ostia, I was watching people streaming past and it struck me that there was a separateness about every individual, even those who were walking along in a group, arm in arm with their friends; they were like people taking part in a funeral procession, all thinking to themselves: 'I'm all right; it was that other chap who died, it'll never happen to me'—as if they believed that everyone else would die, or even that the world itself would end, before anything could happen to them . . . Have you ever been in a funeral procession?"

"Occasionally."

"I have, two or three times. You can understand, then, what I'm trying to say even if I'm expressing it in a rather muddled way: people seem to chase after happiness with that sort of attitude . . ."

"What you are saying is both true and profound."

"My thoughts are probably just the ramblings of a convalescent. But don't you agree that life is becoming more superficial?"

"Not everywhere."

"No, of course not everywhere. I believe that where I live, most people still take life very seriously . . . But on the surface things are drab and horrible . . . You're

47

probably thinking that I'm drab, too, and old-fashioned, dressed like this . . ."

"No, no," Bianchi protested, "quite the contrary."

"I do enjoy life. I like nice things, nice clothes . . . and I should like to wear lipstick and try smoking cigarettes."

"You are the most enchanting girl I've ever met, even in the dress you wear for your vow to San Calogero, even without lipstick."

The girl lowered her eyes, began to trace letters on the window with her forefinger. "What are you writing?" asked the engineer.

"What?"

"On the window, I mean. It looked as if you were writing something."

"Oh, yes, my name. It's something I do automatically whenever I feel embarrassed."

"You mustn't feel embarrassed when I say that you are a beautiful girl and that I enjoy talking to you. It's true."

"Oh," she said, clasping her hands as if to stop herself from writing on the window.

"It's probably not sensible to try to prolong an acquaintance such as ours beyond the limits of the journey, but I must admit that I should like to see you again."

The head of *professor* Miccichè appeared in the corridor; poking out from between the curtains, it appeared to be severed from his body, and sleep and suspicion dripped from it like blood from the head of John the Baptist. "Why did you two slip out?" he inquired with a hint of irritation.

The girl turned to Bianchi. "I should like that too," she said simply. Then, to allay her friend's anxiety, she returned to the compartment.

The train was pulling into Paola, and no sooner had the squeal of its brakes died away than the cries of "*Fragole, fragole*" were heard—for which Miccichè was already prepared with six hundred lire clutched in his hand. He bought a tub of strawberries for each of them, Bianchi included.

The children woke and reached out for the strawberries almost before their eyes were open.

"You and your strawberries!" exclaimed his wife. "Now you've woken the children."

"No I didn't: the shouts woke them up," Miccichè maintained.

"You got up from your seat even before we heard any shouts," said his wife.

"I got up from my seat because . . ." He stopped in confusion then gave an almost imperceptible wink in the direction of Bianchi and the girl. There immediately surfaced in the signora's breast not the tutelary concern felt by her husband but the avowed vocation of every married woman to prod every unmarried one into wedlock, heightened in this particular case by the romance of a long train journey, a professional man from the prosperous north and a nice girl from her own home town.

Nene, who had hardly started his strawberries, announced, "I want some more."

"You can have mine; I don't want any," said his mother.

"Is that or is that not bad manners?" asked his father, seeking support from the company in general.

"He won't even finish his own tub. He talks off the top of his head like you do," said the signora, intending a reproof to her husband for his little gaffe of a moment ago when he had interrupted himself.

"I'll eat mine and yours and then ten more, a hundred more tubs of strawberries," said Nene.

"I'll eat a hundred tubs of strawberries!" mimicked Lulu.

"Two hundred, a thousand," said Nene doggedly; but he was already struggling and a second later he held out the tub to his mother. "I'll finish these later," he said.

"Uh, uh, uh," scoffed Lulu.

"Stop being such a pain in the arse," countered Nene.

"That's not talking off the top of his head," said Miccichè, reasserting himself after his wife's reproof. "That's the language you can expect from a guttersnipe . . . But I'll teach you; I'll pack you off to boarding-school, you'll see."

"With the orphans?" Nene's curiosity was purely academic.

"Just so. With the orphans."

"Unless you die, they won't take me. If you die, then I'll go."

Miccichè turned this way and that in search of some "lucky iron." Clinging to the ashtray and thus protected, he turned to Bianchi as full of paternal pride as ever: "What logic!" And to Nene he said, "Don't fool yourself. They'd take you with your father still alive: a word in the ear of Father Ferraro would be quite enough."

Accurately anticipating Nene's reaction, he leapt to his feet and towered threateningly over the child. "Don't you dare say what you were going to about Father Ferraro, or I'll give you a thrashing that you'll remember for the next hundred years."

"I won't say it: I'll think it," said Nene, quite unruffled.

Miccichè passed his hand nervously over his face once or twice, then laughed. They all laughed. And while they were laughing the ticket inspector arrived; they showed their tickets and Miccichè inquired about arrival times. As soon as the inspector had gone, Nene said conversationally, "I'm still thinking about Father Ferraro."

"My God!" moaned Signora Miccichè. But her husband, Bianchi and the girl laughed until the tears ran down their faces.

They arrived at Villa San Giovanni having discussed Nene's liveliness from all possible angles and quelled a couple of sudden squabbles between the children. Strawberry-colored smears on Bianchi's and Miccichè's shirts bore silent witness to the men's intervention in the role of peacemakers.

Once on the steamer, Miccichè, in great good spirits, suggested that they all go up on deck for a coffee.

"And what about the cases?" asked his wife.

"Ah yes, the cases . . ." said the teacher with a frown. And with the self-denigration beloved of all Sicilians, he explained to Bianchi that as they approached Sicily, it would be a wise precaution never to leave their luggage unattended: conditions here were very different from those in the north of Italy where, Miccichè fondly imagined, suitcases only moved, like dogs, at the behest of their legitimate owners.

Signora Miccichè, who had her own ulterior motives, suggested a solution: Bianchi and Dina should go for a coffee first, and when they came back—and they were to take all the time they wanted—she and her husband would go up with the children.

The protests of the children, who couldn't wait to go on deck, were firmly suppressed. Miccichè, to be sure, was not entirely easy about the plan, torn as he was between his duty to the girl's brother and his natural inclination to further a romance. But his wife's decision settled the matter.

Thus they found themselves alone, the girl and Bianchi, as the first rays of the sun turned the Straits of Messina into shining gold below them. They drank their coffee quickly and then sat in silence facing the compact, gleaming whiteness of Messina.

After their sleepless night, the brilliance of the morning sun upon the water seemed to dazzle their very thoughts. As the ship began to move, the girl said, "Shall we go down? The children will be impatient to come on deck."

The children were more than impatient: Lulu was grizzling and Nene was stretched in silent protest upon the floor.

Seeing Bianchi and the girl, Miccichè pointed scornfully to his son. "Look at that!" he exclaimed. "Is it a boy or is it a dog?" But Nene was already up and away; his mother and Lulu followed him.

Miccichè was already out of the door when the thought that he was about to leave the girl alone with a man on an almost deserted ship pulled him up short. He returned, and more to ease his conscience than allay any anxiety, asked the girl if she would like to come with them. She said no, that she was tired.

"Professor Miccichè is uneasy," said Bianchi.

"He wants to deliver me back home safe and sound," said the girl, smiling.

"I hope he doesn't assume..." said the engineer. "I hope you'll..." He floundered to a halt.

"Yes," said the girl, blushing.

They were both silent and their silence made Miccichè wonder. Was the engineer so gentlemanly that he had dared to say nothing to the girl, or so *un*gentlemanly that he had made a pass at her and been rebuffed? His doubts were resolved by his wife, who, using the mute language of eyes and eyebrows, assured him that the idyll continued but that everything had been perfectly correct; you only had to look at their faces to know this.

Miccichè immediately felt easier, but it occurred to him that, if a romance was really afoot as his wife maintained that it was, then he had a moral obligation to discover more about the man with whom he was dealing. That he was an engineer, a bachelor (or so he claimed), aged about thirty-five, pleasant and seemingly of good character, this he knew already, but he must dig deeper. He asked, "Am I right in thinking that you come from somewhere near Venice?" (Miccichè had done an officer training course in Marostica and recognized the intonation.)

"Vicenza," the engineer replied.

"A lovely city; very civilized place."

"Vicenza, Vincenza, Vincenzina, Aunt Vincenzina," chanted Lulu.

"Aunt Vincenzina's *panedispagna*," said Nene, licking the remains of a bar of chocolate from his fingers.

"And you live in Vicenza?" Miccichè continued his interrogation.

"It's my legal residence, yes, but I only pay a fleeting visit now and then. My mother still lives there, and my brothers . . . I've spent a lot of time away from Italy—America, Iran . . . And now Sicily, at Gela."

"Oil?"

"Oil."

"Well tell me then, in confidence: is it true that there

is oil in Gela, or not?" Miccichè asked, lowering his voice to a whisper.

"Certainly there is oil there."

"Because there are rumors that it might be—how shall I put it?—a put-up job: that the quantity may be so small that the game's not worth the candle."

"That's rubbish!" exclaimed the engineer.

"That's what I say. But sometimes—you know how it is—I get the feeling that they're trying to throw dust in our eyes . . . Don't misunderstand me: the man at the top is a genius, no question about it . . . Even if this Gela business were a swindle, it takes a genius to set up a swindle of that magnitude."

"There's no swindle," the engineer assured him.

"If you say so . . ." said the teacher, raising his hands in a gesture of surrender. And, dropping the subject of oil, he returned to that of more immediate interest, Bianchi himself.

"Are you staying long in Gela?"

"I expect so: if not in Gela itself, then in Sicily anyway. Troina, maybe, or Gagliano . . ."

"Do you like Sicily?"

"I think I shall like it very much. I've never been there before," said Bianchi with a glance at the girl.

"How about that?" said Miccichè to his wife and the girl. "He's been halfway round the world and has never been to Sicily! Jesus Christ, these people from the north are all the same!"

"But I've always meant to go to Sicily," said Bianchi apologetically.

"Of course, of course! 'The land of golden oranges that glow in foliage dark,' " Miccichè quoted with bitter irony.

"It happens to everyone," said his wife, defending Bianchi and at the same time hoping to take the edge off her husband's resentment. "People put things off saying that they'll do them next year, and sometimes next year never comes, and they never even manage to see the places they've always longed to see, or, if they do, it's by pure chance. We ourselves, for instance, have never been to Piazza Armerina, yet my husband has been planning a visit ever since we were married."

"It's quite true," agreed her husband. "It does happen. But whenever I meet someone as old as this gentleman . . . Forgive me, what is your age?" (Miccichè was not losing sight of his primary objective of gleaning every possible scrap of information about his traveling companion.)

"Thirty-eight."

"That a man of thirty-eight should have never been to Sicily, well, I don't mean to be offensive, but that does tend to make me see red . . . Because what happens (I am of course speaking generally) is that strangers come along, knowing nothing about the place or the people but only seeing things in terms of their own so-called 'boom' or economic miracle, and feel free to carve up our poor Sicily any way they please . . . So personally I don't give a fig for this 'boom'; your 'boom' is at Sicily's expense, you are frying us in our own fat . . . For pity's sake let's change the subject."

Lulu and Nene had shouldered imaginary machine-guns and were firing salvoes of "boom-boom-booms" at each other.

"He was a separatist," said Signora Miccichè in order to explain her husband's heated words.

"Independent," Miccichè corrected her. "And I still am."

"You have your oil now," Bianchi said by way of consolation.

"Oil? Believe me, they'll soon grab it," said Miccichè. "Do you remember Musco in Martoglio's *San Giovanni*? He kept an oil lamp burning before an image of the saint until a neighbor came along and used the oil; so when the real devotees came to worship, the lamp was dry. And that's what will happen to our oil. One long pipeline from Gela to Milan and they can just drain it off . . . The devotees, those who have the interests of Sicily at heart, will be left wringing their hands . . . I'd rather not talk about it."

"But if this happens, either now or in the future, won't Sicilians, too, be to blame?"

"Certainly: it's a Sicilian failing to stand around and wait for the ripe fruit to fall off the tree straight into our mouths."

"Then, forgive me, but if that's the case, I can't see what you would gain by becoming independent."

"We're not all like that," said the girl. "The fact is, that we like to make others believe the worst about us, like people who imagine that they are suffering from every illness under the sun and find some relief in talking about it."

"True enough," said Miccichè, slightly abashed. But he brightened up almost immediately at the sight of the sea off Taormina. "What a sea!" he exclaimed. "Where else would you see anything like this?"

"It looks like wine," said Nene.

"Wine?" repeated his father, perplexed. "What on earth's the matter with the child's eyesight? He doesn't seem to be able to tell one color from another. Does the sea look wine-colored to anybody else?"

"I don't know: it does seem to have some dark reddish streaks in it," said the girl.

"I've either heard the expression before or I've read it somewhere: 'A sea the color of wine . . . dark as wine . . . ,' " mused Bianchi.

"Some poet may have written that maybe, but I've never seen any wine-colored sea," said Miccichè. And to Nene he explained: "Look: just down here, by the rocks, the water is green. Further out it is blue, a deep blue."

"To me it looks like wine," said the child confidently.

"He's color-blind," pronounced Miccichè.

"He's nothing of the sort," argued his wife. "He's just obstinate."

She too attempted to convince Nene that the sea was green and blue.

"It's wine," said Nene.

"See how obstinate he is?" said his mother. "He is now declaring that the sea actually is wine."

"Just a moment," said Miccichè, pulling his tie down from the luggage rack. It had green and black stripes. He showed it to the child, asking him, "What color is this tie?"

"The color of wine," Nene replied decisively and with an impish grin. Miccichè threw the tie in the air.

"You may as well give up. He's just being obstinate," said the signora.

"Perhaps he's color-blind as well," persisted Miccichè, but without conviction.

"Wine-dark sea: where have I heard that before?" Bianchi wondered. "The sea is not the color of wine; Miccichè's quite right. Very early in the morning, maybe, or even in the sunset, but not at this time of day. Yet the child has stumbled onto something. Perhaps it's the effect, almost like the effect of wine, which a sea like this produces. It isn't drunkenness, but it overpowers the senses, harks back to some ancient wisdom . . . Eduardo De Filippo ought to recite the Dialogues of Plato—in Neapolitan . . . But this is Sicily, and perhaps it's not the same."

The railway line ran parallel to the most glorious sea that Bianchi had ever seen: at times the swaying of the train gave him the impression of being aboard an aircraft taking off, the landscape all tilted to one side along the flight path.

Miccichè, to whom the posing of alternatives seemed a habitual figure of speech, asked, "Is that beautiful or is it not?"—gesturing towards the Aci coastline as if it were a painting he had just completed.

They all agreed that it was indeed beautiful—except Nene, who was totally absorbed in removing the safety pins that held in place the strips of linen that served as antimacassars.

"Is Nisima on the coast?" inquired Bianchi.

"Unfortunately not," replied Miccichè regretfully. "It's in the arid Sicilian hinterland ... Nevertheless, it has a beauty of its own, nothing as breathtaking as this, but the kind of beauty that grows on one, particularly in the form of nostalgia when one is away for a time ... Here the beauty is so obvious that it would dazzle even an idiot; it takes more time and more perception to appreciate the beauty of Nisima ... It's a different thing altogether."

"Is there a local Mafia?" asked Bianchi.

"Mafia?" exclaimed Miccichè with the same incredulity he would have displayed had he been asked whether the inhabitants of Nisima had webbed feet. "What Mafia? All nonsense!"

"Then what about this?" asked Bianchi, holding out his day-old newspaper and pointing to a headline that screamed across four columns: "Mafia Says No to Dams."

"Absolute nonsense," retorted Miccichè again.

Bianchi mused: "Here's an educated man, kind, courteous, a good father to his children; and he refuses to speak about the Mafia, is even surprised that one should mention it, as though to do so were to give undue importance to something trivial, a mere bagatelle. I'm beginning to understand something about the Mafia. Chilling."

The train drew into Catania. "Catania," Miccichè announced. "The end of the line for this locomotive; it stops here."

"I'm getting out: I want a little walk," said Nene.

"They're going to move the carriages onto another line now, so you'd better stay put," said his father.

"I want a *granita*, a *granita* and some biscuits," said Nene.

"Me too. I want a *granita* and some *brioches*," said Lulu.

They had *granita*, biscuits and *brioches*.

"They call this stuff *granita*?" said Nene disgustedly, but only when he had drained (partly onto his clothes) the last mushy drop. "Don Pasqualino makes real *granita*. As soon as we get to Nisima, I shall drink a bucketful!"

"This is better than Don Pasqualino's," said Lulu for the sake of argument but without conviction.

"You don't know anything about it. This is made from water, lemon flavoring and sugar; Don Pasqualino uses real lemons and he puts egg-white in it too," Nene explained knowledgeably.

"He knows it all," said his mother. "He's inquisitive about everything, always asking questions . . ."

"I'm not inquisitive. Aunt Teresina's inquisitive."

"Now you're saying nasty things about her!" said his father triumphantly.

"You're always saying: She's so inquisitive, the old witch."

Stung, Miccichè threatened the boy with a tremendous back-hander. Nene, totally unimpressed, explained for the benefit of the two non-family members of the party: "Aunt Teresina is rich and she's going to leave all her land to us. But I don't give a . . ."

The slap came from his mother.

"Aunt Teresina's going to leave her land to me," said Lulu.

"That's enough!" shouted his father.

"Aunt Teresina's got a wig. Aunt Teresina's got a squint . . ." chanted Nene.

"You ought to be ashamed of yourself!" said his mother.

"Aunt Teresina won't give you any more *ciambelle*," said Lulu.

"*Ciambelle* covered in mold: it makes me feel sick just to think about them." His masterly impression of vomiting earned him another slap.

To comfort him, the girl offered to take him for a walk along the corridor. Nene accepted, saying, "I'd be better off out of here, where you can't talk sensibly."

But seconds later, he came rushing back alone, glancing over his shoulder as if he were being followed. He sat down and held an open newspaper in front of his face. The impression that he was reading it was spoiled by its being upside down. A marshal of the carabinieri loomed in the doorway, gigantic, corpulent and with an ugly, scowling face rendered even more ferocious by the heat and by the rivulets of sweat that coursed down it. Nene eyed him from behind the paper. The marshal inquired if this were the right carriage for Agrigento, thanked them and went on down the train. Nene, lowering the paper, emerged from behind it like an actor taking a curtain-call; but he emerged to the jeers of Lulu and the laughter of the rest of them. Weeping with rage and mortification, he bit Lulu, chewed his knuckles and kicked his feet; then gradually, still sobbing, he fell asleep.

A discussion arose about the upbringing of children, and of a child like Nene in particular. The parents maintained that Nene was undisciplined, and for this they blamed themselves and also the Sicilian environment; on the mainland, they said, children were brought up better and were better behaved. Bianchi and the girl, on the other hand, maintained that although Nene's language left something to be desired and his reactions tended to be violent, he undoubtedly possessed a lively intelligence and a ready wit, and his nature was generous. Miccichè and his wife clung to their point of view, though with a certain archness, and finally allowed the full tide of their affection to flow over the sleeping child.

As the train traveled on through the sun-baked, deserted landscape, they were like figures in a nativity scene grouped around the slumbering child, with their honest affections, their faith in life. Surely all this friendship, all this love must endure beyond the chance encounter, the shared journey, thought Bianchi, believing that he had at last penetrated the very core of life, epitomized by the essential goodness of this Sicilian family. He could, he mused, prolong it for a lifetime with this quiet, serious girl of few words and profound feelings; he had to say something definite to her before they separated, even accompany her home, speak to her parents. But when Miccichè began to reach down the cases because they were about to arrive in Canicattì, he told himself he was no longer a child, that there was a time and a place for everything and that he would be able to spend his first free day on a brief visit to Nisima.

They began to say their farewells long before they arrived at the station, renewing them on the platform where the diesel for Campobella, Licata and Gela was already waiting. They were all much affected—except for Lulu, who did everything in his power to distract the girl. Nene invited the engineer to go with them to Nisima, promising him one of Don Pasqualino's *granitas* and an evening at the club. Bianchi, his eyes on the girl, promised Nene that he would come soon. The child hugged him. Miccichè gave him his card.

From the train, where he had taken a seat near the window, Bianchi watched them as, laden with luggage, they made their way to the exit.

"I shall go to Nisima this coming Sunday," he decided.

But as the train moved off, all his emotion of sorrow and of love was immediately blotted out by sleep. Just before he drifted into unconsciousness he had a vision of the face of the man who had advised him to take this particular train, to travel in this particular carriage: the face wore a sadistic, satisfied expression. "Lord, what a trip!"

THE TEST

ONE LITTLE PILE of counters, each the size of a one hundred lira coin, to be sorted into three stacks: the roughest, the less rough, the smooth.

One length of wire and a pair of pliers to twist the wire into the shape of a triangle.

One sheet of card with circles on it, arranged rather like a bunch of grapes, each circle containing a number. As many as possible of these numbers had to be read off, from a certain distance away, starting when the man holding the watch said "Go" and finishing when he said "Stop."

The words for "go" and "stop," *via* and *basta*, were the Italian words that the man pronounced best. A tall man with pink cheeks, blue eyes and fair hair that grew away from a double-crown. A Swiss from Zurich, Blaser by name, he was in Sicily to recruit female labor—girls between the ages of eighteen and thirty—for a factory producing electrical goods, meters apparently, though his Italian was so limited that it was difficult to tell.

He might have been Catholic, Lutheran or Calvinist. The priests gave up trying to work it out. He conducted his examinations of the girls in a quiet, detached manner, either in the presbytery or in the vestry itself, as if these surroundings had long been familiar to him from experience as a choirboy or attendance at Sunday school.

He traveled around the province from one town to another in a car with a driver, hired, after a meticulous examination of the contract and a suspicious haggling over the price, from the provincial capital; a city in the very heart of Sicily, unfriendly, isolated and exposed to winds that plucked it like a Jew's harp.

The driver had come to take a keen interest in the whole business of the examinations, following it closely in the presbyteries and vestries, and sometimes he could not resist putting in a word for a girl who had failed the test or was not the right age, even though the Swiss invariably ignored all such interventions.

The same scene was played out everywhere they went. Even the girls seemed the same from one place to another, and the priests too. At the agreed hour, the priests would be waiting for Mr. Blaser, and about twenty girls, usually accompanied by their mothers, would have gathered in the vestry or in a downstairs room of the presbytery, whispering excitedly or giggling nervously. The parish priest introduced them with assurances of their observation of the Christian faith and their possession of the domestic virtues that would be transmuted, in Switzerland, into the virtues of the good worker. Mr. Blaser produced his counters, wire, pliers and sheet of card and the tests began.

Despite the good money he was earning and the easy, pleasant way in which he was earning it, the driver's satisfaction was marred by twinges of remorse: he felt like an accomplice in some kind of rape of the Sabine women mysteriously concocted by a northerner—and a German at that—and the Sicilian priests. He had no love for the Germans, having suffered a long period of privation in one of their prisoner-of-war camps, and he had no love for priests, for a variety of reasons. The few words of German that he had managed to pick up when his stomach was aching with hunger, now enabled him to translate his client's name into *blower*, and in vengeful fantasies he imagined the man naked and suspended, his cheeks puffed out and breath issuing from his mouth in a bundle of spikes—just like the plaster cherubs in the churches. The vindictiveness was fueled by Mr. Blaser's attitude towards the driver: he treated him like a part of the car and any attempt at conversation or any intervention on behalf of a girl was dismissed as an irrelevance, as unwelcome interference. This was humiliating enough, but when, at the slightest attempt at familiarity, *the blower* looked at him as if he were an inanimate object, an object that had the surprising and unwelcome faculty of speech, the driver's sense of humiliation boiled over into hatred. He felt humiliated, too, by his own conflicting sentiments. Emotions of such complexity seething within the breast of a man to whom he was paying a fair wage for a job of work, and aroused by that very job itself, would have been unimaginable to Mr. Blaser; but even had he realized their existence, he would have felt only contempt.

A week went by in this way; a dozen towns and villages visited, about a hundred girls recruited; no problems, no hitches. Until the day for which Mr. Blaser had scheduled a visit to V., an isolated town surrounded on all sides by an arid landscape, a farming town where the communal land had by now been eroded by partition and where the Mafia flourished.

During the journey, the driver recounted some of the events that made up the recent history of the town, padding his relation with all the most lurid details. The Swiss gave no sign of either interest or surprise.

Arriving in the center of the town, where the priest was already waiting on the steps of the church, the driver was locking up the car while Mr. Blaser and the priest exchanged greetings, when a young man approached him. The driver responded to the youth's initial salutation, then the two stood looking at each other for a few moments without speaking, the lad evidently timid and tongue-tied, the driver conscious of a sudden sinking of the heart, for the stories he had been relating to Mr. Blaser were now acting like a yeast to his sense of apprehension. To hide his anxiety he adopted an arrogant tone as he demanded brusquely: "What is it?"

"Something," said the boy, "that you must do for me."

The driver thought: "This is it," but without any idea of what "it" might be.

"If I can," he said with a hardness of tone that meant to convey his decision not to accommodate the boy; or at least, should he do so, it would be out of kindness, certainly not out of fear.

"You see," said the boy, "it's about a girl, a girl who wants to go to work in Switzerland . . . I don't want her to go, you see . . . She's in there now, with the priest . . . They mustn't accept her, that's all . . . I don't want that . . . We're going to be married, you understand . . ."

"I don't understand at all, my friend, and it's none of my business. My job is just to drive that chap around. I'm only the driver: he pays me and I drive him wherever he wants to go. About what he does, I know nothing and care less. Everyone has his own job to do. I do mine and he does his. There's really nothing I can do." His tone was gentler now; he felt sorry for this young man, a child on the brink of tears.

"You must help me," said the boy.

The driver was thinking: "I feel really sorry for him . . . and in a town like this they'll go to any lengths . . ." He heaved a sigh of annoyance and embarrassment.

"O.K., I'll see what I can do. But remember that my word counts for nothing. That chap is a Swiss, a German Swiss. You know how pernickety the Swiss are: they make watches and they work precisely like watches ... And as for the Germans, they don't bear talking about ... Hearts of stone. Ever tried to get blood out of a stone?" And he walked off towards the church. But at the threshold he paused and turned again to the boy, who was still standing at the foot of the steps. His look was both reproachful and sympathetic.

"What the hell's her name?" he asked.

"Rosalia," said the boy. "Rosalia Calaciura."

In the vestry, Mr. Blaser had already unpacked his things and was laying them out upon the long table with care and delicacy, like surgical instruments. Indeed, the whole impression given by Mr. Blaser as he worked in the sacristy sliced by great swaths of sunlight streaming from the high, barred windows, under the ambiguously ascetic and sadistic faces of the bishops and archdeacons that gazed, highlighted by the sunshine, from the faded canvases above the massive cupboards of dark walnut wood, in the curious redolence of mingled wax, vanilla and mustiness, was that of a man preparing for some grim surgical operation or a session of torture. The girls watched Mr. Blaser's hands with fascination; as did the priest.

The strained, anxious atmosphere was shattered as the driver entered the room calling: "Mr. Blaser, may I have a word with you?" Mr. Blaser turned round, surprised, almost indignant, his eyes even colder than usual. The driver beckoned to him. Mr. Blaser puffed out his cheeks in annoyance ("the blower," thought the driver) and moved insultingly slowly.

"Do you understand the kind of town this is?" the driver whispered in his ear.

"I understand," said Mr. Blaser.

"Mafia: a Mafia stronghold," said the driver.

"I understand."

"You know what the Mafia's about?"

"I couldn't care less," said Mr. Blaser, pronouncing the words laboriously.

"I could," said the driver. "And if you want a word of friendly advice, I suggest you think very carefully indeed before you say you 'couldn't care less.' The difference between caring and not caring about it could well mean the difference between life and death."

"I don't understand," said Mr. Blaser; and in that very moment he did begin to understand, a little.

"So listen carefully to what I have to tell you," said the driver.

"Get on," said Mr. Blaser, meaning: get on with whatever it is you have to say, I've no time to waste.

"Among these girls there is one that you must not accept. Her name is Rosalia Calaciura."

"I must not accept her?"

"No. Reject her, reject her immediately. No good."

"Wrong age?" asked Mr. Blaser. "Or . . ." He tapped his forehead to indicate mental deficiency.

"No, no," said the driver impatiently. "She's all right as far as that goes; but still you must not recruit her, that's all."

"All?"

"That's all." The driver clenched his fist, then opened his thumb and first finger at right angles to each other and tapped the finger with the thumb three times as if firing a pistol. "Bang-bang-bang: you, me and the girl . . . They'll bump us off."

"Who will?"

"The girl's boyfriend, the one who doesn't want the girl to go away."

"Ah!" exclaimed Mr. Blaser, and turned his back on the driver.

"He'll take her," thought the driver, "I know it. Out of arrogance and sheer bloody-mindedness; and to spite me. And if I were in the shoes of that poor devil who's waiting outside, I'd teach him a lesson. As things are, he'll blame me. Nothing will convince him that this man's just plain pig-headed; he'll think I refused to speak up for him."

The tests were now under way. The driver concentrated on trying to discover which, among all those girls, was Rosalia Calaciura. There were fourteen candidates. He singled out the three prettiest. One he heard immediately called by another name. That left two, but neither was Rosalia.

Rosalia was not pretty at all; at second or third glance, some might have found her attractive, but certainly not pretty. She was short and dark. And in the test, she proved to be one of the brightest.

As soon as Mr. Blaser had called out "Stop!" at the end of Rosalia's test, he glanced towards the driver. The latter shook his head. Mr. Blaser stood there for a moment, hesitating. He turned to the priest.

"I don't want any trouble," he said.

"What?" said the priest, surprised.

"Trouble, headaches, unpleasantness . . ." said Mr. Blaser, pronouncing the words badly but revealing an unsuspected richness of vocabulary.

The priest's head swiveled on his embroidered collar as if on a pole; his eyes started from his head and his mouth hung open; like a character in a comic strip, one could almost see the bubble containing an exclamation mark over his head.

"This girl is engaged to be married?" asked Mr. Blaser.

"No," said the priest, beginning to understand.

"No," said Rosalia's mother.

"I say that she is," said Mr. Blaser.

"They're not engaged," said Rosalia's mother. "There's a boy who wants to marry her, an unemployed layabout. But my daughter does what I tell her."

"It's not true that he's a layabout," said Rosalia. "He hasn't been able to find work."

"He's out to ruin you," said her mother.

"He doesn't want to ruin me; he's in love with me . . . That's one of the reasons that I want to go to Switzerland, so that I can earn the money for my dowry and get married."

"It's all very well to be thinking about a dowry," said her mother, rising, "but what about the poverty at home? Have you forgotten how we're counting on the bit of money you'll be able to send me from Switzerland?"

"Of course I'll send you something; but I'm going to Switzerland to earn my dowry."

"Enough," said Mr. Blaser. "I'll take her."

The driver left the vestry and walked through the empty church. The boy was waiting for him, leaning against the car.

"I warned you," said the driver.

"Did he say he'd take her?"

"I might just as well have kept my mouth shut . . . Obstinate as a mule . . . Moreover, he as good as said that you were trying to make waves. The mother was angry, she said that you were a good-for-nothing who was trying to ruin her daughter's life. But the girl defended you."

"She loves me," said the boy.

"She loves you—and she's going off to Switzerland," said the driver sarcastically.

"A full belly never believes an empty one," said the boy defensively.

"Mine's not that full," said the driver. "I only meant that it was up to you to stop her applying for this job in

Switzerland in the first place, or coming along today to take the test. If she still wanted to go ahead, it means she must have had her own reasons: either she loves you rather less than you think she does, or she's fed up with being poor."

"She is that," said the boy.

"So, if you really love her, let her go ... She'll come back; she's a very determined young lady, she'll come back ... And then you can marry."

"If only I could find work ..." the boy said.

"You will: with so many people going away, there shouldn't be any shortage of work for those who stay behind."

"The fact is, that as more people go away, the town becomes poorer."

"That can't be right," said the driver, who saw the economy in terms of simple arithmetic.

"It isn't like a lot of people packing and squeezing themselves onto a bench, where if one gets up the others can spread out and make themselves more comfortable ... Here, no one is sitting down, and if some go away, the others don't even notice it; or the only thing they do notice is that the town is becoming deserted."

"It all sounds very complicated," said the driver.

"It is complicated," the boy agreed.

"Then why don't you go to Switzerland too? Switzerland or Germany ... Germany's right next door to Switzerland."

"I've already been to Germany. I was there for three months . . . But this is how I see it: a man isn't an animal. He can survive in a country not his own, even though it hurts him to be separated from all this." He gazed around him at the church, the piazza and up at the sky ablaze with a golden sunset—"But his dignity, his basic human rights are things that no one should take from him."

"Rights? Why, didn't they pay you?"

"Oh yes, I was paid: the money in my Friday pay-packet was always correct to the last *centesimo*; no cheating, no mistakes. No, I'm talking about another sort of rights, the kind of rights that enable you and me, even though we hardly know each other, to talk man to man, as equals . . . With them it's different: they don't seem to see us, that's what I mean, they just don't seem to see us . . . It makes you feel like a fly in a spider's web, dangling over one of those glasses of beer . . . The beer! Dear God, the beer . . ."

"Indeed!" said the driver, feeling an icy chill run down his spine at the memory.

"Now you see why the thought that she'll have to go through all this like I did, is driving me crazy. Switzerland won't be any different."

"She's a woman," said the driver, "and women are adaptable. They can easily change their ways and feelings . . . A woman can be cleaning out a stable one day, and the next time you see her she's a fine lady."

"That's true," said the boy.

"Shall I tell you what I think? It's all a matter of destiny. Whether she goes to Switzerland or not, if it's your destiny to marry her, you'll marry her; if it's your destiny to lose her, you'll lose her."

Mr. Blaser came out of the church, the girls swarming out after him.

"I'll be off then," said the boy, "and thanks all the same."

"Not at all. Good luck," said the driver.

Mr. Blaser walked over to the car.

"Primitive place," he said.

جا

GIUFÀ HAS BEEN living in Sicily since Arabian times. In the script of that period his name appeared as a small, crested bird, its tail stuck straight up in the air and a grape in its beak جا A thousand years later, Giufà still shambles along the roads, ageless like all simpletons and up to all kinds of mischief. And sometimes people are exasperated by him, sometimes they laugh at him indulgently, and sometimes, as they lounge on the steps of the church the way they used to on the steps of the mosque, they cluster round him, putting foolish ideas into his head and solemnly telling him the tallest of tall stories. His mother, a poor widow, relict of a man scarcely less stupid than his son but who had at least worked like a donkey, leaves her home every now and then to look for Giufà, and taking his hand, she drags him home with all

the feeble strength that remains to her; for the last thing
that Giufà wants is to stay at home, but when he is out
his mother, in her anxiety, seems to hear a cricket that
chirrups into her ear: Giufà, Giufà, Giufà, جا, جا, جا.
What trials he has brought to the old woman throughout
his one thousand years of life! Blows that would have
killed any other mother, shocks that would have turned
a hundred heads white, tears enough to fill a river. And
the forces of law and order forever knocking at the door,
every variety of them from representatives of the *quaid*
and the viceroy to companions-in-arms of King Ferdinand
and carabinieri serving under King Vittorio. Like the time
Giufà killed a cardinal and got away with it either by
sheer cunning or sheer stupidity: for the two are closely
allied, and Giufà, stupid as he was, could also be extremely cunning. Or the time when Giufà, in swatting
a fly on the face of a judge (and a high-ranking judge at
that) dealt such a blow that the great man turned a triple-
somersault and knocked himself out; and when he came
to, he would have had Giufà impaled but Giufà, as always, got away with it. Many are the tales that could be
told about Giufà. None, however, can equal the tale of
the cardinal, which nearly led Giufà and his poor old
mother (completely innocent as she was) to the gallows.
In fact Giufà, in his madness, was also innocent. For it
was the idlers who amused themselves by filling his head
with nonsense, and dangerous nonsense at that, who per-
suaded him to go hunting with the ancient harquebus

that belonged to one of his ancestors—or maybe one of his descendants, who knows, for where Giufà is concerned years and even centuries have no chronology—and which hung, along with its powder-horn and shot, its flint and wadding, on the wall at the head of his bed. Giufà welcomed the idea and asked eagerly about loading the weapon and the business of hunting, about which animals to kill and which of them were the tastiest. They explained everything, fitting their instructions to their own purposes as well as Giufà's. The tastiest, they said, were those with red heads; and by this they meant the birds that the country folk call redcrests and which are, in fact, skinny little bundles of bones that no hunter would ever bother to shoot. No sooner said than done: Giufà only waited until his mother had gone off to early Mass first thing in the morning before he took down the harquebus, loaded it with all the powder, all the wadding and all the shot and betook himself to a likely spot just outside the town. It was a pleasant spot with leafy hedges, flowers everywhere and pools reflecting palm-trees whose fronds stirred gracefully in a delicious breeze. Giufà saw big white birds with long necks gliding over the water and others with shining colored plumage stalking majestically along the gravel paths, trailing fan-shaped tails that seemed to be studded with eyes. But Giufà was watching for one thing only: a red head; though whether it would belong to a bird or an animal such as a hare or a donkey or even to something that looked like a man, he had no idea, but only that it must have a red head, any living creature that had a red head. So he waited, with the heavy weapon all but pulling his arm out of its socket.

And sure enough, at last he saw, moving slowly along behind and above one of the leafy hedges, an object that was red: a beautiful red, a glowing red, a red with a silky sheen to it and shaped like a little dome on a mosque. It was moving, so it had to be a head, and the animal that it belonged to had to be big enough to feed a regiment; not that Giufà was stupid enough to want to feed others with the fruits of his own labors; indeed he was already planning to eat the tripe first, prepared as his mother did it with herbs and spices, to make a good meat broth with the head and to quarter the rest of the carcass and pickle it in brine. He lit the fuse and aimed at the little red dome. The report put the cannons of Castellammare to shame and the kickback left Giufà sitting in the middle of a streamlet. Rising, he rushed to the point where the little red dome had disappeared behind the hedge. His kill, he discovered, was good and plump, red all over, and had probably been shaped very much like a man (two fat white hands, two feet encased in black shoes with silver buckles) though, in the state to which it had now been reduced, this was impossible to judge. There was food enough for a month. He slung the carcass over his shoulder, raced home and deposited it on the kitchen table. His mother had not yet returned from church. "What a lovely surprise for her," thought Giufà. "She will be happy; and now that I have provided her with the fat of the land, she will never again be able to call me a lazy good-for-nothing."

It was a surprise that very nearly cost his mother her reason. She tore her hair, beat her head against the wall and wept. "You've killed the cardinal," she wailed, "you've killed the cardinal!" Giufà, who had no idea what a cardinal might be, was totally taken aback by her reaction. He had been expecting a celebration, and now gazed on this ecstasy of grief, his eyes round with surprise, totally at a loss as to what he should do. Then suddenly, because he too was capable of bursts of temper at times, he slung the body of the cardinal over his shoulder again, marched outside and threw it into the well in the courtyard.

His mother continued to wring her hands and to moan. And Giufà was still raging; but we shall never know whether from rage or calculation, stupidity or cunning, he seized the ram his mother was rearing and that was at that moment grazing among the weeds in the courtyard, raised it above his head and hurled it, too, into the well. Moaning more loudly than ever, his mother ran into the courtyard; but the ram was drowned already. To escape her lamentations Giufà hurried away from the house.

News of the cardinal's disappearance spread rapidly in the town and throughout the whole of Sicily. Soldiers searched everywhere for him, rummaging with their pikes through stores of straw and grain, through piles of stones and heaps of manure; they even searched inside the mattresses of the poor, when they were not too poor to own mattresses. And they offered a handsome reward of one hundred silver florins for information leading to the discovery of the cardinal, alive or dead, and ten times that sum, one thousand florins, for denouncing the man responsible for his disappearance. On hearing this, the snoopers and the money-grubbers took to weaving up and down the streets like so many shuttles on a loom, and their ears, constantly distended to catch the lightest whisper in the streets or in the houses behind closed doors, seemed to stretch to the size of trombone bells. It was thus that the captain of the guard, the leader of the patrol, came to hear about the stench of putrefaction issuing from the well in the courtyard by Giufà's house, and, with an impressive body of men, went to investigate. Giufà himself was in no way implicated.

One by one, after the captain, the men approached the well and retreated rapidly, nauseated by the stench. Despite the tenderest of feelings towards the cardinal, not one amongst them aspired to being lowered into the well to haul up a body that was all too obviously in an advanced state of decomposition. Each one approached the well, glanced quickly at the water reflecting his face and polished helmet and then backed away hurriedly to fill his lungs with the sweet morning air. So, when the captain noticed Giufà standing quietly beside the well, apparently oblivious of the smell but absorbed solely in the sight of so many men in gleaming halberds and breastplates moving about the courtyard, it was only natural that he should be struck with the idea of lowering him into the well. For a florin Giufà would have dived into the water head-first.

The point is not mentioned in any of the sources, and therefore there is no way of telling whether Giufà remembered what he had done. Only a few days had passed since he had thrown the bodies of the cardinal and the ram into the well, but it is generally held that idiots have no memory, or at best only a confused, dreamlike recollection of things past. In any case, he was in high spirits as they attached ropes around his waist and under his arms and lowered him into the water. When he stood on the bottom, the water came up to his chest. He knelt down and it came nearly to his mouth; he began to grope around under the water. Almost immediately he gave a shout: "I've found it!"

"His Eminence?" asked the captain, holding his nose tightly between finger and thumb.

"What eminence?" asked Giufà.

"I mean the cardinal," explained the captain.

"I've never seen a cardinal," said Giufà, "much less touched one, so what I've got here might as easily be a cardinal as a dog."

"Imbecile!" roared the captain. "Maybe a good hiding would teach you the difference between a cardinal and a dog."

"If you threaten me," responded Giufà, "I shan't lift another finger; you can come down and see for yourself whether this is a cardinal or a dog."

"I was joking," said the captain.

"That's better," said Giufà, groping away under the water, his face turned upwards with the perplexed expression one sees on the faces of the blind.

"Get a move on," said the captain.

"Ah! Here's something hairy, or perhaps woolly. Was the cardinal covered with wool?"

"I don't know," said the captain.

"You don't know...Do you know how many feet the cardinal had?"

The captain seemed to have been attacked by a swarm of wasps: he began to dance around, waving his arms in the air.

"How many feet did His Eminence have? You dare to ask how many feet our beloved cardinal the archbishop had? Pull him up," he said to his men, "and I'll give him such a hiding that he'll be crawling on all fours for the rest of his life."

The soldiers did not pull him up; had they done so, one of them would have had to take Giufà's place. And, apart from that, the captain himself, who in the heat of the moment had forgotten to hold his nose, found the stench a strong argument in favor of moderating his tone. "Look," he said, "let's stop playing games."

"Who's playing games?" Giufà inquired. "I don't know what a cardinal is: all I want to know is if whatever it is we are looking for had two legs or four."

The captain, momentarily confused by exasperation, said: "Four."

"Two, sir," said his men in a chorus.

"Would I have said four?" said the captain, turning upon them. "Why is everyone trying to drive me crazy? I said two, and any oaf who dares to suggest otherwise will get what's coming to him, that's for sure."

"You did say four, you know," said Giufà, smiling and wagging a finger at the captain in playful reproof. Then he became serious again. "So tell me: was it two or four?"

"Two," said the captain, fuming.

"This has got four: so it's not the cardinal," said Giufà.

"Two or four," said the captain, "tie it to the rope and we'll haul it up."

"But why do all that for nothing?" said Giufà. "If it's not the cardinal, we're wasting our time."

"Do as I say," said the captain, "and you'll have nothing to regret."

Giufà continued to grope beneath the water as if he had not heard. And then: "Wait!" he shouted triumphantly. "Did the cardinal have horns?"

"Horns . . . ? His Eminence . . . ? Did you say horns?" yelled the captain, and began to run in circles around the well screaming: "Sacrilege! Sacrilege!" gnashing his teeth and beating his fists upon his breastplate.

"Are you sure?" asked Giufà calmly.

"I'll roast you like a sucking pig!" shouted the captain, glaring down into the well.

"Can't I even ask a question?" said Giufà. "If you'd only tell me what a cardinal looks like, I wouldn't need to ask any more questions."

"What a cardinal looks like?" yelled the captain. "He looks like you or me, imbecile!"

"Nothing different? Nothing special?" pursued Giufà.

"Nothing," said the captain.

"Then why are so many people looking for him?"

"Because he's a very important man, like a prince."

"Is he rich?"

"Extremely."

"And what does he wear on his head?"

"A kind of skull-cap, a red beret."

"But not horns . . . You are sure about that?"

"Absolutely," said the captain, quivering with rage.

"But just a moment . . . For the sake of argument," said Giufà, who, up to his waist in water, was as cool and fresh as if he had been sitting in an arbor of flowers, "You say he didn't have horns, and I believe you . . . But you only saw him when he was alive. How do you know that he didn't sprout horns after he died? . . . I know that if a man is wicked, he grows horns after he dies. Did the cardinal commit any grave sins?"

The captain's rage exploded anew into curses and threats. When he calmed down, Giufà's voice came from the bottom of the well, inquiring ever so softly: "Not even one tiny little sin as small as this?" And he indicated the tip of one nail.

"Not even one tiny one," said the captain.

"And what work did he do?"

"Work? What work, idiot? He was the cardinal. He was in charge of the priests, all the priests in Sicily."

"Don Vincenzo too?" asked Giufà. Don Vincenzo was the priest of his parish.

"Don Vincenzo too," replied the captain patiently.

"So if you ask me," said Giufà, "this cardinal of yours might well have grown horns. I'll send him up and you can see for yourselves."

Working under water, he attached the ropes to the body he had been exploring and then shouted to the men to haul away. And into the light rose the soggy, decomposed corpse of the ram, and Giufà with it. The captain and the soldiers watched, dumbfounded.

"Well, is it the cardinal or not?" Giufà inquired merrily.

The captain let fly at him with his boot. And that was the only punishment Giufà received, because it never occurred to anyone to search the well for a second time.

DEMOTION

HE REACHED HOME, as he did every evening, at eight o'clock precisely, after his usual session of *perdivinci* at which, since he had won, he had lost two hundred lire.

As his partner in this four-handed card game he had been saddled with Nicola Spitale: a champion at every other game, especially *quaranta*, when it came to *perdivinci* he might as well be tucked up in bed with the lights out, for, on his own admission, the game made him so sleepy that he couldn't keep his eyes open; he sat there gazing at his cards from beneath drooping lids with a fixed, vacuous expression.

"There are," he thought, "some games which I dislike and which I find boring, so, if I'm asked to play, I refuse. He, on the other hand, will sit there yawning his head off and playing like a moron; yet never, ever will he refuse a game of *perdivinci*!" The ill-temper that had been accumulating in the breast of Michele Tricò vented itself thus in dark thoughts about his friend Nicola, and he was so preoccupied with reminiscences of the game that he did not immediately notice the darkness and silence of the house; he went round turning on all the lights and only when he reached the last one, in the kitchen, did he remark the absence of his wife.

"Filomena!" he called—and heard, from the direction of the bedroom, a small thump followed by a rustle. Entering the room, he heard another rustle, coming from beneath the bed. "Why would she be under the bed?" he puzzled, raising a corner of the coverlet. It was the cat, who immediately began to meow pathetically, starvedly.

"Where can she have gone? . . . And at this time of night? . . . Perhaps her mother's been taken ill and has sent for her." He imagined his mother-in-law on her death-bed. It was high time. A wiry old woman, eighty-five or more, and vicious, poison-tongued, pernickety and capricious.

"I'll go and see," he decided. He turned off all the lights again, then went downstairs and out of the door, which he locked securely. "Of course we'll be obliged to stay all night, and that's just what I need with my cold . . ." He headed towards his mother-in-law's house at the other end of town.

But the old lady was not only in perfect health but

as lively as a grasshopper, the beady eyes glittering, the
tongue as ready as ever. She released the remote control
latch from upstairs, came out onto the landing and, before he had had time to mount the stairs, brusquely demanded to know what he wanted.

"Is Filomena with you?"

"No, she isn't," replied the old lady; then, in dismissal,
"Shut the door firmly or it won't stay shut."

"She's not at home. Where can I find her?" Michele
persisted.

"She'll be in church," said the old lady, withdrawing
and switching off the light. Michele slammed the door
behind him with a noise like a cannon shot. "In church?
What would she be doing in church at this hour? There's
no service at nine o'clock at night!"

The church of Santa Filomena was just round the
corner from where he lived, and he had had to walk from
one end of town to the other to get to his mother-in-
law's, to say nothing of the bile he had to swallow every
time he saw her. "Filomena's going to get a piece of my
mind: she'll never want to go to church again for as long
as she lives."

There was quite a crowd in front of the church. "Must
be something special; perhaps they've invented a new
service, a nocturnal mass; they must be running out of
ideas." As he drew closer, he noticed that the carabinieri
were present in strength. "Must be a major celebration;
maybe the bishop's there."

Someone shouted his name: "Tricò!" It was the brigadier.

"What is it?" Michele asked. He was thoroughly annoyed and quite disposed to pick a quarrel with the brigadier or with anyone else.

"Are you joining in the protest on behalf of Santa Filomena?" inquired the brigadier ironically and with a hint of menace.

"What protest? What's all this about Santa Filomena?"

"What? You don't know anything about it?" asked the brigadier, still ironic, still threatening and now also incredulous.

"I'm completely in the dark," said Michele, with such patent sincerity that the brigadier was convinced.

"It's the women," explained the brigadier. "They're all in the church and they refuse to come out. They're afraid that the statue of Santa Filomena is to be removed from the altar and they say that they're going to stay in there until the archdeacon promises that it will remain where it is."

Michele mused: "Now I understand: the Santa Filomena saga. People have been talking about it for weeks. But what are the priests up to, and who's behind them? The church is dedicated to Santa Filomena, there's a weeklong festival in her honor every year with a fair, torchlight processions, cavalcades, fireworks that rock the buildings, honey cakes and all the rest—and then, out of the blue, comes an edict to the effect that Santa

Filomena never existed!" Aloud he said: "I'm going in to fetch my wife."

"Do . . . If you can . . . If only all the husbands would come to fetch their wives . . . We have a real problem here, Tricò my friend." The brigadier's smile was friendly and encouraging. He had believed that the communists were involved in some way for the following reason: that very morning he had had to give orders for the removal of a poster which had been pasted overnight to the base of Garibaldi's statue bearing the following legend, in red and black letters like those found in the rubrics in a missal: *Martyrologium Romanum: Apud Septempedanos, in Piceno, sanctae Philomenae Virginis*—each letter a full hand's-breadth high. The beauty of it was that he had seen the poster but had assumed that it was something to do with the church, advertising a day of prayer, maybe, or a crusade against blasphemy, and had attributed its unusual position, right at the feet of Garibaldi, to a whim on the part of the archdeacon—until he received a telephone call from the archdeacon himself, around eleven o'clock, protesting that the poster was an obscenity and was causing the chapter grave anxiety about the Force's loyalty to the Church. The brigadier had pointed out that no one in the entire division, from the marshal down, had a word of Latin and that he, personally, knew not a thing about Santa Filomena. The poster was, however, removed, both the brigadier and the archdeacon agreeing that responsibility for it, in all probability, lay with the communists.

That Tricò, the head of the local communist cell, had been so obviously in total ignorance of the affair, was therefore a matter of profound relief.

Michele entered the church—in a manner of speaking, because as soon as he got inside the door he found himself squashed against the wall like a flat fish. "Jesus Christ! Are there really this many women in town?" he wondered. And how on earth was he to find his wife in this press of women and children? Apart from anything else, the church was almost in darkness, the only meager source of light being a few candles in front of the altar and the oil lamps hanging before the Stations of the Cross. An inspiration on the part of the archdeacon or the brigadier, turning out the lights; but any poor devil who came to look for his wife was presumably expected to provide himself with a lantern. And as if the darkness were not enough, there was also the wailing of babies to contend with, and the acrid smell of sweat, damp clothing and fenugreek. "I'm getting out of this. A quick bite at the trattoria, then home to bed . . . And when she's sleepy enough and hungry enough she'll come—and I'll give her a piece of my mind." But his sense of pique was too strong: that his wife, his own wife, should be involved in a seditious act, and all over Santa Filomena! He began to push his way through the throng shouting, "Let me get through, Christ Almighty!"—an expression sufficiently shocking to produce an instinctive recoil which gave him a free passage. Among the faces which parted before him like the waves of the Red Sea, he noticed that of his niece Filomena. She had her baby at her breast.

"Where's Filomena?" he asked her.

"Down at the front, near the choir."

Front row, as in the theater, he thought. But to his niece he said, "Take that child outside: he'll suffocate in here." A murmur of disapproval greeted his words, but his niece did not move. He continued to push and shove his way towards the altar and when he finally reached it, leaned, exhausted, against the rail. From above, Santa Filomena looked down upon him; like most statues, she had the kind of eyes that follow you around no matter where you move, but her gaze was placid and benign, unlike that of the statue of God the Father in Monreale which seemed to pierce you with red-hot needles. "Santa Filomena does not exist . . . she never has existed." With this thought he tried to rid himself of the childish feelings of devotion and fear which were awakening within him. He turned his back on the altar and scanned the front rows of women. He could not see his wife among them and as he searched, the faces began to dance before his eyes in the dim, flickering light of the candles wavering in a draft— another tactical move by the archdeacon, probably— which threatened to extinguish them completely from one moment to the next. The draft penetrated his shirt and he felt the sweat chilling on his skin.

Suddenly he saw his wife, her face swathed in a black veil as if for a funeral, her eyes turned fearfully towards him.

"Hoping I wouldn't spot her," he thought, and went towards her, raging inwardly but outwardly totally calm.

"Come on home," he said.

"I can't," said Filomena. "We're staying here until we have the archdeacon's promise that the saint will remain on the altar."

"Come on home, I said."

"I'm not coming."

"I see . . ." said Michele. Despite his coldly menacing tone, he was actually at a loss, trapped in the kind of situation that teeters between tragedy and farce. His wife's revolt had opened a chasm in his vision of the world, a vision in which Major Herman Titov, orbiting the earth in his spacecraft, encountered the departed spirit of the Michele Tricò who had died, aged ninety, in 1929 and from whom his grandson Michele had inherited, besides the name, that eminently right-minded view of women in general and wives in particular upon which Michele senior had acted throughout the years between Garibaldi's landing and the signing of the Concordat, with a consistency vividly remembered not only by the family but by the entire town. "Good for one thing only," had been Grandfather Michele's opinion of women, pronounced at a time when the old man was no longer able to avail himself of this advice, and the little boy playing at his knee, ever ready to refill his pipe or fetch him a glass of water, had as yet no way of understanding it.

"I'm not coming," Filomena repeated.

"Your mother . . ." said Michele. An idea had suddenly occurred to him: he would play a little trick on his wife, a trick which would pay her back for her rebellion and also pay his mother-in-law back for her treatment of him.

"What about my mother?" Filomena asked, immediately alarmed.

"Oh nothing," said Michele, shamming the embarrassment of one who bears grave tidings but wishes to use the utmost tact in their communication. "Nothing to worry about."

"What has happened?" Filomena almost shouted the question as she leapt to her feet.

"I've told you, it's nothing to worry about . . . Come to think of it, you may as well stay here: after all, the doctor's there, and the priest . . ."

"The doctor! the priest! . . . Then it must be serious!"

"A slight stroke, she's lost her power of speech, that's all." And to himself he added: "If only it were true!"

Filomena turned to the women near her. "Did you hear that? My mother has had a stroke; I must go at once." She worked her way to the end of the row. "We must hurry," she said to her husband. She turned to the altar where Santa Filomena stood and crossed herself apologetically before starting to make her way out. Michele looked again at the saint with her white robe, golden girdle and the green palm-frond in her hand. "Just like an extra in *Quo Vadis*," he thought.

Their passage through the crowded church was made easier by Filomena's repeated justification of her defection: "My mother has had a stroke; I have to hurry," at which the women sympathetically made way for her. But before reaching the door, Michele paused to renew his warning to his niece Filomena as she rocked her baby (who was now crying) in her arms and crooned a lullaby. He said to her brutally: "By all that's holy, that child is going to die—as a sacrifice to the glory of Santa Filomena!" The words caused a wave of indignation.

"Blasphemer!" they shouted at him.

"You're the blasphemers, for rebelling against the Pope!" Michele shouted in reply as he slipped through the door with his wife. Bathed in sweat and with his ears burning, he paused on the threshold of the church to get his breath back.

"Congratulations!" said the brigadier. "You did it."

"I did it all right," said Michele, "but it's hell in there . . . Believe me, there's only one solution: leave them to stew in their own juice."

"I couldn't agree more . . . But I have to obey orders . . . We'll see . . ."

"Good luck," said Michele.

"Come on!" urged Filomena impatiently.

"You seem to be in a great hurry all of a sudden," Michele remarked conversationally, strolling along behind Filomena with the air of one enjoying a leisurely promenade.

"Of course I'm in a hurry! My mother . . ."

"Talking of your mother, I'm surprised you didn't drag her along too to strike a blow for Santa Filomena . . . She might have had a real stroke then, finding herself in that hell-hole!"

"Then it's not true!"

"That she's had a stroke? No, of course it's not true. The idea occurred to me for the very fact that I saw her only half an hour ago and she was in much better health than I am."

"I know you'd like to see her dead and buried, the poor old lady; but what harm has she ever done to you?" asked Filomena tearfully.

"You know as well as I do, what she has done to me . . . What interests me much more at this particular moment, however, is what *you* have done to me this evening . . . Knowing my views, what on earth made you go along there to join in with that rowdy mob?"

They had reached home by now and Filomena was already busying herself about the kitchen, preparing supper with unwonted speed.

"It wasn't a rowdy mob; it's your lot that's the rowdy mob . . . Ours was a silent demonstration. They want to take away our saint, so we stayed in the church to guard her . . ."

"Ignorant woman! You're as stupid as a donkey!"

"I know that the saint has always been here, that she has protected this town and performed miracles, that masses have been celebrated for her and three-day vigils . . ."

"And so what? All that it means is that some fool once misread a tablet in the catacombs and thought that the bones of a virgin called Filomena were buried underneath it. And he was wrong: the inscription meant something completely different . . ."

"I don't believe it . . . What about the miracles? How do you explain those?"

"They're a load . . ." Michele clapped a hand to his lips to stop himself from uttering the obscenity that was on the tip of his tongue. "Well, never mind, they're not the real problem; what we do need to establish is if you and all the other poor misguided fools who staged this demonstration are actually Catholics or not."

"Of course we're Catholics!"

"Then, when you were informed that Santa Filomena never existed, your duty was to put your tails between your legs and creep away with no fuss . . . When the priest tells you that you'll go to hell if you don't vote for the Christian Democrats, you believe him; yet when he tells you that Santa Filomena never existed, you stage a revolution . . . You're all mad!"

"You don't understand anything about it!"

"I don't?" Michele exploded. "It's because I do understand that I'm trying to explain it to you in a way you should be able to grasp . . . But if you won't listen, then all I can say is that you're totally naïve, and this whole affair is absolutely ridiculous . . ."

As she tossed handfuls of cabbage into boiling water, Filomena wept silently over the cross she had to bear in the shape of a husband who believed neither in God nor in the saints.

"You should be crying over your own abysmal ignorance."

"The miracles . . ." Filomena insisted rebelliously, "the miracles are facts. No one can deny the miracles . . ."

"They're the biggest joke of all, the miracles . . . I can remember your mother having a dream about Santa Filomena, that she was holding up three numbers; your mother played those numbers in the lottery and won. A saint who revealed numbers on a lottery ticket was funny enough, but then there was an even more ridiculous incident when some priest had visions of Santa Filomena and they nearly canonized him for it. I can't remember his name, some French priest, I recall . . ."

"You see? There are proofs!"

"Give me strength! Santa Filomena, you idiot, does not exist; it was the Pope himself who told you that . . . And what reason could the Pope have, in this instance, for telling you a pack of lies? Starting a revolt? Santa

Filomena does not exist and there's an end to it. And the beauty of it is, that the French priest and your mother and dozens of other priests and dozens of other women, have all seen a nonexistent saint as clearly as I see you."

"She does exist," said Filomena, as immovable as a rock.

"She does not exist and she never has existed," said Michele, "and they will take her down from the altar and put another saint in her place and you will continue to light candles and have masses said and to vote as the priest tells you to ... And your mother will win another lottery with the numbers dictated to her by the new saint ... Until someone comes along saying that yet another misguided fool has misread yet another inscription ..."

He left the kitchen and went to sit by the table waiting for Filomena to bring him his plate of cabbage with a boiled egg. He took the newspaper from his pocket, as he did every evening, and began to read. He had only just remembered his paper and was now kicking himself for wasting time over a futile discussion with a woman—for arguing with a woman is like washing a donkey's face—when he could have been peacefully perusing his copy of *L'Unità*, the communist daily. He glanced at the headlines: "Observatories worldwide record explosion of Soviet 'superbomb' in Novaya Zemlya. General disarmament!" "It'll come," he thought, "now that they all know that we have a bomb more powerful than theirs." He read on: "XXII Congress of Communist Party of the USSR votes to remove Stalin's tomb from the Mausoleum."

"My glasses!" shouted Michele. "Bring me my glasses!" He needed them to read the smaller print. Filomena brought them quickly.

Michele became absorbed in his paper, oblivious of the steaming plate of cabbage on the table before him. *Cont. P. 9 Col. 3.* He rifled frantically through the paper in search of P. 9 Col. 3 and found it: ". . . that Stalin was to blame . . . acknowledged that it was no longer reasonable to preserve the tomb of Stalin in the Mausoleum . . . Resolution put to the vote. Delegates raised their red order papers. The motion authorizing the removal of Stalin's body was carried unanimously."

Michele Tricò threw the paper violently towards the ceiling; the sheets fluttered down, some onto the sewing machine, others onto the floor.

"What's the matter?" asked Filomena.

Michele stabbed his fork into the cabbage on his plate. His wife watched him anxiously, fearing a return to the subject of the saint.

"Nothing," said Michele. "Nothing at all."

PHILOLOGY

"DO YOU THINK it comes from the Arabic?"

"Very likely, my friend, very likely... But the study
of words is far from being an exact science: where they
come from, how they get into the language, the changes
of meaning that they undergo—it's all very confused...
And this is one of the words that has given rise to
more various, and more idiotic theories than most; very
scholarly theories, very closely argued, but often very silly.
The fact is that everyone tries to establish the current
meaning of the word before establishing its origin, and
this is where the problems start; someone who maintains
that the word refers to a mental state, goes off in one
direction, while someone who maintains that it refers
to an actual thing, goes off in another... Here's Petrocchi, who spells the word with double-f in the Italian

way: 'An association of people from all classes of society and from all walks of life, who lend each other assistance regardless of legal or moral principles.' He relates it, though very uncertainly, to the Old French word *mafler*, hence *maflé* and *maflu* meaning 'to eat, to cram oneself with food' . . .″

"Not very nice."

"It quite turns your stomach . . . 'to eat, to cram oneself with food.' What a strange mentality! And it is a question of mentality: such a connection would never have occurred to a man like Pitré, a little old man who looked as if he never ate at all, as light and skinny as a bird. I can remember him; he used to live in the same neighborhood; died during the First World War. Listen to what Pitré writes on the subject: 'The Mafia is neither a sect nor an association, it has neither rules nor statutes. The *mafioso* is not a thief nor an evil-doer; and although the term has come to be applied in recent times to the thief and the evil-doer, the reason for this is that the public, not all of whose members have a high standard of education, has not had time to consider the significance of the word nor to observe that, to the thief and the evil-doer, the *mafioso* is simply a clever and courageous man and astute with it, in which sense it becomes necessary, even indispensable, to be *mafioso*. Mafia implies a consciousness of self, an exaggerated concept of the power of the individual as sole arbiter of every conflict of interests or ideas; from this derives the inability to bear with the superiority, and even more, the authority of others. The *mafioso* expects respect and nearly always offers it. When crossed, he does not appeal to the law, to public justice, but takes matters into his own hands and, should the remedy be beyond his own power, he will call on the assistance of like-minded friends.' "

"He writes like an angel."

"Maybe; but not without certain illogicalities."

"Really? To me that seemed as clear and accurate as the Gospel."

"You read the Gospels?"

"Just a figure of speech . . . But I've heard them read sometimes."

"Do you know what the Gospel says? *Unto him that smiteth thee on the one cheek offer also the other.* Is that how you react?"

"If someone smites me, I gun him down."

"So . . . Even the Gospel contains some illogicalities . . . But let's return to Pitré . . ."

"I've got it; I've spotted the fly in the ointment. First he says that the Mafia is not an association, then later he says that *mafiosi* help each other, so there has to be some kind of association."

"Very clever; but you must learn to express yourself properly. It's not done to say things like 'I've spotted a fly in the ointment' when speaking about a great man, a literary giant."

"It's only a figure of speech."

"You must watch out for, and avoid, figures of speech, sayings, proverbs. You must speak concisely, correctly, with tact and courtesy."

"God Almighty! D'you think I'm an educated man or something? The nearest I ever got to university was looking after sheep!"

"If you let slip an expression like 'God Almighty' in front of the Commission . . ."

"But do you think they'll actually call me?"

"I'm dead sure of it. Why on earth do you think that I'd be wasting my time on you if I were not certain? Of course they'll call you."

"It makes me break out into a cold sweat just thinking about it."

"How many times have you been interviewed by the police, or appeared before a magistrate?"

"Water under the bridges. They haven't bothered me for over ten years now . . . And anyway, this is something new, the Commission I mean. Who knows how they'll operate or what questions they'll ask? The police and the magistrates always ask about a particular event, a particular person; they want to know if I was involved, if I had anything to do with this person or that, and where was I on that evening at that time . . . You can prepare yourself for questions like those and then simply trot out the answers . . . But, from what I've heard, the Commission can ask what it likes; and you've got to be pretty quick on the uptake, and pretty cool . . ."

"Have I ever let you make a mistake, take a false step, say anything stupid?"

"No. Never."

"Well stop worrying then ... Just so that you know what is going on, I intend to appear before the Commission too."

"You?"

"Yes, my friend, I myself. I too have my small contribution to make."

"But ..."

"A contribution to confusion, naturally ... And I guarantee that the moment will arrive when they won't know what's happening to them, what with history, philology, anonymous letters ... Have you any notion about the number of the anonymous letters that will be sent to the Commission? When the Americans made me mayor in 1943, I got something like a thousand of them. Judging from those letters, a whole town had turned to spying; even Panebianco, the Deputy, who had been in prison until Mussolini fell from power. These same letters were sent on to the Americans. To begin with, they took them at their face value; they arrested a few people and sent them to Orano. Then the letters began to flood in at such a rate that even they got the message ... Imagine what will happen this time ... This is a country, my friend, where the left hand doesn't trust the right hand even if they both belong to the same man ... You'll see ..."

"That's true."

"Let's return to the subject . . . According to Fanfani . . ."

"Why do you still bother about Fanfani?"

"Not Amintore, you ass; I'm referring to Pietro Fanfani, the compiler of an Italian dictionary. In this dictionary the word *maffia*, with a double-f, is defined as 'a Sicilian secret society' and he derives the term from the Arabic *maehfil*, signifying both a meeting and the place where it is held. Zimbaldi, Rigutini and more or less everyone else takes the same view until we come to Palazzi . . . I shall read you Palazzi's definition; it will amuse you. The first part is taken direct from Petrocchi, then he continues: 'The Mafia's objectives are not invariably evil, but the means employed are illegal. Membership of the Mafia was at one time widespread in Sicily.' Most amusing."

"I like it, especially when he says that the Mafia's objectives are not invariably evil. There speaks an honest man."

"Rather, one who has relied upon other honest men. But the really amusing phrase is: 'at one time widespread in Sicily.' "

"That's what we say, too: the Mafia doesn't exist anymore . . . Even the Minister said it once . . ."

"The Minister, like us, is not the compiler of a dictionary . . . And just think, this was printed in 1948 . . . 'At one time,' indeed! In the time of the dinosaurs, no doubt! And now we come to your actual Sicilians, learned Sicilians. The first Sicilian dictionary to include the word was Traina's, in 1868; and it describes it as a new term, possibly derived from the Tuscan *smaferi*, meaning police spies, villains . . ."

"I don't like that."

"You'll like this even less, when he goes on to say that in Tuscany the word *maffia* signifies extreme poverty, and 'the most extreme form of poverty is that poverty of spirit which seeks self-aggrandizement through the exercise of brute strength, for brute strength implies brutality which, by definition debases its user to the level of the beasts.' How do you like that?"

"It stinks."

"But he adds: 'Self-assurance, the appearance of courage, boldness.' "

"Now he's beginning to make sense."

"However, not to dwell at too great a length upon etymology, et-y-mol-o-gy, that is, the origin of words, we'll only take one more example, that of Father Gabriele Maria da Aleppo, Capuchin missionary and teacher of Arabic, who concludes his learned analysis thus: 'From the foregoing definitions, it would appear that the term *mafia* originally signified, on the one hand, *protection from oppression, immunity from social restraint, remedy for any injustice suffered, strength, physical robustness, serenity of mind and acknowledgment of and gratitude for benefits received*; and, on the other hand, *the best and most exquisite aspect of anything*, which is entirely consonant with the definition given by Pitré.'

The source-words that Father Gabriele suggests are these, from the Arabic: *mohafat*, meaning to defend; *hofuat*, the best aspect of anything; *mohafi*, a friend, specifically a grateful friend . . . I've simplified slightly to avoid confusing you."

"This Capuchin certainly knew what he was talking about."

"Maybe, but I'm not convinced. Fanfani is much more convincing."

"Fanfani? Is he one of us now?"

"You must pay more attention, my friend. I've already told you that this Fanfani is nothing to do with the politician . . . You obviously have not been attending to my explanations."

"The fact is, to be honest, that this is all rather a waste of time. God Almighty! What am I supposed to do with all this learned stuff about words? I carry all the wisdom I need, all the wisdom there is, packed into my wallet and my double-barreled shotgun."

"Then Traina is correct: your opinion of yourself depends solely upon your ability to use brute force, you're like an animal . . . But I don't give a brass monkey: I'm not the one who's out on a limb; I can leave you to take what's coming to you. Why not, since you and your friends carry your wisdom packed into your wallets, and double-barreled shotguns and cars loaded with dynamite . . . And your wisdom has now been enriched, has it not? with dynamite and T.N.T. And this mess is the result . . . Leave that sort of thing to the Germans in the Tyrol; they're the fanatics, the madmen. Fascists . . ."

"The dynamite worked, though, didn't it? Even you, in the beginning . . ."

"Let's get this straight. In the beginning, as you said (and I don't remember exactly when it was) you and your friends came to me and said that it was time to find a substitute for the shotgun because everyone was talking about shotguns and the place was becoming identified with them and we were getting a bad reputation abroad; and there were, you said, better methods, quicker, surer, and, when accuracy was the name of the game, it would be advisable to use them; and, you said, you knew a certain young man who was an absolute genius with explosives. So I let you get on with it, you and your genius; a genius who left the car without defusing the package . . . Some genius!"

"You know what happened: a moment of panic, a second's distraction . . ."

"Distraction! Distraction that produced a complete shambles, that brought the world down about our ears— with the result that you now see."

"But I did get someone to make a phone call, to tell them not to touch the car or all hell would be let loose."

"And they still opened the car . . . Did you honestly think that they would not? Because of an anonymous phone call that could quite easily have been a hoax?"

"I'm sorry, but it happened and there's nothing we

can do about it. I was sorry for the soldiers; they were just unfortunate victims."

"They were all unfortunate victims, all those who got killed. And the worst of it was, that I had to attend the funerals."

"Not for the first time."

"You seem to be getting a bit above yourself."

"Me? With you? I wouldn't dare!"

"Good. But these terrorist methods have got to stop. We're not anarchists, we believe in order . . . And when there are accounts to settle, we'll settle them from now on in the time-honored ways."

"But the lads were getting really keen . . ."

"It was all very spectacular, I'll give you that . . . But that road's the wrong one . . . Or do you think we should be starting to work on our own atom bomb? . . . We've got to be discreet; we need brains, preparation, tact . . . Our only problem at the moment is the Commission of Enquiry; let's tackle it with a cool head . . . So: Pitré says that the term *mafia*, whatever its origin, and even though it was only mentioned for the first time in 1868 . . . In which dictionary was it mentioned first?"

"Traina's."

"Well done . . . Even though it was only mentioned for the first time in 1868, was in use before the arrival of Garibaldi . . . And we know that the thing itself, the association, was already in existence by the fact (this is my addition) that the *mafiosi* imprisoned in the Vicaria issued a directive in 1860 addressed to their friends outside, advising them to behave well and not commit such crimes as theft, rape and murder that the Bourbons could use as a general argument, as propaganda, as we would say today, against the Garibaldi revolution . . ."

"I didn't know that."

"There are a great many things which you do not know and which you would do well to learn . . . Culture, my friend, is a wonderful thing."

END-GAME

THE DOOR OPENED, taking him by surprise, while his finger was still hovering over the bell-push. "Come in," said the woman, with a smile, "I was expecting you." And there was a trill in her voice as if she had indeed been anticipating this moment with eagerness and joy. There must be some misunderstanding, he thought, and tried to calculate the consequences as he stood on the threshold feeling anxious and somewhat at a loss. She must have been expecting someone, he thought, someone she didn't know at all or knew only slightly, or had not seen for several years. All the more likely since she was not wearing glasses and he knew that she usually did. "You were expecting me?"—"Of course I was expecting you . . . But do come in, please." The voice still trilled.

He entered, taking three steps over the floor of ceramic

tiles patterned to represent an antique nautical chart, moving slowly, heavily, as if wading through mud. He turned to the woman, who, still smiling, waved him towards an armchair.

To clear up the misunderstanding and find out what was happening, he asked: "But whom, exactly, were you expecting?"

"Exactly?" she echoed with a smile that was now ironic.

"You see, I . . ."

"You . . . ?"

"In short, I think that . . ."

"That I must have taken you for somebody else." The smile had vanished and she looked younger than before. "On the contrary, it was you that I was expecting. True, I'm not wearing my glasses, but I only need them for close work. I recognized you when you were at the gate. Now, perhaps, at such close quarters, I should put them on again; then neither you nor I need be under the slightest misapprehension." The glasses were resting on an open book, the book that lay on the window-sill. So while waiting for him, her ears no doubt strained to catch the creak of the gate, she had been reading; but she had read only a few pages. He was conscious of a sudden, ridiculous curiosity to know what book it was, what kind of reading matter she had chosen to while away the time of waiting. But why on earth should she have been waiting for him? Had he fallen into a trap? Was he the victim of deception? Or had the man who sent him been seized by remorse?

Oddly enough, the glasses with their thick, black rims made her appear younger still; her eyes, dilated by the lenses, looked slightly surprised, slightly fearful. But she was neither surprised nor afraid. She even turned her back on him as if in defiance. She opened the drawer of a writing desk and took out some papers; when she turned and came back towards him she was carrying a sheaf of photographs. "They're a bit blurred," she said, "but there's no mistaking them. This one was taken at eleven o'clock in the morning on the twenty-first of June in Via Mazzini: you are with my husband. This one was taken at five in the afternoon, in Piazza del Popolo on the twenty-third of July: you are alone, locking your car after parking it. And your wife, too, is in this third one ... Would you like to see them?" Her tone was ironical but without animosity, almost amused. Now at last he felt ready for what he had to do. And yet he couldn't: from what he had so far managed to piece together, he understood that he could not, should not, go through with it. He indicated that he wished to see the photographs. She handed them to him and stood looking at him with the half-anxious, half-complacent expression of someone showing photographs of the family, of the children, and awaiting the inevitable compliments. But the man was as if paralyzed, all perception, thought and movement sluggish, distant, hopelessly weighed down. And the compliment came from her, banal and violent: "You know, you're really photogenic!" And in fact the blurring in the photographs nowhere succeeded in obscuring his identity, whereas his wife and the Commendatore had fared worse.

"Do sit down," said the woman, waving him again towards the nearest armchair. He sank into the cushions as if among the ruins of his world. She asked: "Would you like a drink?" and, without waiting for a reply, fetched a bottle of cognac and two glasses. He found himself clutching his glass while the woman, sitting opposite him, sipped at hers and regarded him with amusement. He drank, then looked around him like a man recovering from a heart attack. Nice place. He gave her back the photographs.

"She's a pretty girl, your wife. Had you noticed the resemblance to Princess Grace of Monaco? I may be wrong; the photograph isn't very clear. Am I wrong?"

"Possibly not."

"So it hadn't struck you!" Again the dreadful trilling laugh. "Are you in love with her?"

He said nothing.

"Don't think I'm prying; I'm not asking out of mere curiosity."

"Then why did you ask?"

"You'll see . . . Are you in love with her?"

He repelled the question with a gesture of his hand.

"Either you refuse to answer, or I am being given to understand that you have no special feelings regarding your wife."

"Whichever you prefer."

"I prefer a definite reply," she said, her tone hard and menacing. Then it changed to one of persuasion, of sorrow: "Because, you see, I must know beforehand if you can take what I have to tell you."

"Before? Before what?"

"You have already answered my question."

"I hardly think so."

"Oh yes. I said: I have to know beforehand if you can take what I have to tell you. And you, instead of asking what you were supposed to take, what revelation was coming about your wife or about your love for her, leapt at the word 'before.' Quite right. You are not worried on your wife's account but on your own. Quite right. That's how it should be."

"I'm asking you now: what am I supposed to take?"

"What I am about to tell you."

"About my wife? And you're worried as to whether I can take it?"

"About your wife. And I was worried about your reaction because we two are destined for a long, close friendship and the air has to be cleared first. Always assuming, naturally, that you agree."

"But my wife . . ."

"All in good time. Meanwhile, tell me if you have understood."

"If I have understood what?"

"The photographs, the fact that I was waiting for you. Have you understood?"

"No."

"Don't disappoint me. If you have really not understood, all my hopes are dashed. And yours too."

"Mine?"

"Of course. Did I not say that we were going to be friends? Then tell me honestly: Have you understood? . . . And don't be afraid to speak, there are no hidden microphones here, no tape-recorder running. You can always look for yourself, if you want to . . . I'm about to ask you to do something that is simple, quick and profitable—and without risk. Not to mention that I am saving you from an immediate and certain danger. You must admit, then, that I have the right to ascertain your degree of intelligence at least . . . Well then, have you understood?"

"Not completely."

"Naturally . . . Tell me what you have understood so far."

"I have understood that you know."

"A brief and comprehensive reply. Do you want to know how I found out?"

"I should be interested."

"We're using up precious time, but it's right that you should know. But when do you have to meet my husband? I'd like you to tell me straight away, because our future friendship depends on this meeting with my husband this evening. What time is it to be?"

"We haven't planned to meet."

"So you still don't trust me. I know my husband very

well indeed, and it is inconceivable that he would not make an appointment for this evening. What time?"

"A quarter past midnight."

"Where?"

"A country lane about thirty kilometers from here."

"Good, then we have time enough . . . But perhaps it would be better if you asked me some questions now."

"I wouldn't know where to start; I'm rather confused."

"Really? I had expected you to be sharper than this, a man of lightning reflexes and snappy judgments. But perhaps the reason for so much surprise and bewilderment is that my husband told you nothing about me, about my character and about my ability to divine his most secret thoughts. After fifteen years of marriage, a man like him is an open book for a woman like me. A very stupid, very boring book. What do you think?"

"About what?"

"About my husband."

"Judging from the position I'm in at the moment, he must be an idiot."

"I'm happy to hear you say that. But you should have realized earlier what an idiot he is. I do understand, however, how you must have been dazzled by his imposing presence, his *savoir-faire*, the aura of wealth that he creates by spending money continually though with a certain shrewdness, a certain nonchalance . . . Oh he really is wealthy, don't be alarmed . . . As far as all that goes, I, too, fell for it. Not that I regretted it: my one real disappointment was in having married him for love, so to speak, instead of interest. But I would have married him anyway; and my eyes were swiftly opened. And I not only adapted myself to it, but actually welcomed a state of affairs that allowed me to gratify every whim, capricious or malicious, a state of affairs that gave me everything a woman can desire, including contempt for the man she lives with. And now the idiot's gone and ruined everything."

"I can't think, however, that he is the complete idiot you take him for. As far as this present business is concerned, certainly he has behaved stupidly and carelessly . . . But he is a self-made man, or so he gave me to understand, and that is certainly the general opinion. And he has achieved wealth, power . . ."

"Your idea about self-made men comes straight out of romantic fiction or American manuals on 'How to Succeed.' But I can assure you, from my knowledge not only of my husband but of a fairly large number of 'self-made men' that they have all without exception been 'made' by other people, who in their turn have been 'made' by a set of circumstances, coincidences and sordid little deals that, even if the result seems a story-book success, remains fortuitous and meretricious . . . In the last war my husband fought with the Fascists alongside Sabatelli, who became Minister for Public Works; they were both volunteers. And that's the long and the short of it. And you cannot imagine how stupid Sabatelli is. In a well-ordered and honest society, where no papers were forged and men had to depend upon their own merits and abilities, the most favorable of circumstances would have carried them both to the threshold of public office—as door-keepers; the most unfavorable would have carried them over the threshold—of a prison. Instead of which . . ."

"Instead of which, they have become wealthy, power-ful and respected men . . . But you invited me to ask you some questions. May I?"

Irritated at being stopped in the middle of her oratori-cal flow, she gave way but with bad grace.

"There are many things that I am curious about, but what intrigues me most is this: Why were you expecting me on this particular evening?"

"Because today, over lunch, my husband asked me if I was planning to go out this evening to see a film or visit a friend, explaining that he would be home late, very late, as he had some committee meeting to attend. He has already had two such meetings this summer, so the third had to be the vital one: vital for him, mortal for me. With-out even pretending to a profound knowledge of him, anyone who knows my husband at all well is aware of his superstitious feeling for the number three, which, for him, is the perfect number. Where nine's concerned, of course, he becomes completely ga-ga. The third meeting, then, the third of the month, and you arrive on the dot of nine o'clock. It was he, was it not, who told you to ring the doorbell on the stroke of nine?"

"Yes, but I thought . . ."

". . . that it was a detail carefully calculated by his meticulous mind. You cannot understand how little of the meticulous there is in his mind—always supposing that he has one. And I should be most surprised if your being a teacher of mathematics had not played quite a part in his selecting you for this . . . shall we say delicate? . . . mission. He barely knows the multiplication tables, but is obsessed with the idea that his own misappropriations, and all successful robberies, depend upon mathematics in its purest form. In certain bank robberies he hears the music of the spheres, no less. Robberies as reported in the papers, timed to the second, perfect . . . And when they fall short of perfection, he studies the reports, analyzes the weak points and the mistakes and mentally perfects the whole operation. He did that on one particular occasion a few years ago. There'd been a crime that you must have read about: the trial made headlines. My husband was so enthralled by it that he got to the stage where he would send one of his employees to the courtroom every morning to secure a seat, just in case he should be able to make the time to go himself later in the day; and, more than once, he did make the time. But while he was busy spotting the mistakes that had led the defendant to the dock, he was in fact making one himself. If you . . . In short, if everything had gone according to plan, at least ten people would have remembered his interest in that case, especially the clerk who kept the place for him and one of the tribunal whom he knows very well and who used to smile at him from the bench from time to time."

"Was that when you began to be suspicious?"

"I had had my suspicions even earlier, but it was his enthusiasm about that trial that made me realize that he was formulating an actual plan of action."

"So then you got in touch with the firm of investigators."

"It took a long time and cost a great deal of money, but, as you see, it was worth it. For a couple of years all the agency did was send me reports on his infidelities. That made me laugh: his infidelities! I had been completely indifferent to them since only a few months after my marriage. He had always bought women, he went on buying women, he bought me with marriage, believing that the price, although substantial and long-term, was bearable."

"And it turned out to be unbearable?"

"I suppose so."

"I mean, why did it become unbearable?"

"It was my fault, naturally. I did everything I could to push him away from me, to push him to the edge of my life, of my days, of my nights. It was a very narrow edge, consisting simply of a stream of checks . . . No, there were no other men. Or rather, that only happened once, by way of an experiment when I first began to feel a real repulsion towards my husband. The experiment failed. So don't start getting ideas."

He flushed angrily, seeking a violent retort.

"Don't be offended. I'm quite aware that I am neither young nor beautiful. You might even accuse me of being old and ugly. But I wanted to avoid your fooling yourself into thinking that you might be able to get all my money, instead of just a part of it, by using my living body after disposing of my husband's dead one. I want everything absolutely clear between us from now on."

"Then you admit that not all the blame is on your husband's side."

"I admit nothing; and if you, at the point you have now reached—the point we have both reached—now choose to weigh up the pros and cons of the two courses of action that are open to you, to go along with my husband's plan or with mine, and to balance one against the other in the scales of St. Peter, that's your business. But it would be most unwise. You"—she smiled as if paying him a compliment—"are a small, greedy crook. If you bite off more than you can chew, you'll end by choking yourself."

"I'm no crook."

"Really?"

"No more than you are."

"Agreed. And much less of one than your wife, I should say."

"Possibly. But why do you say that?"

"I deduced it from what I know. Did you know that your wife, as one says, goes with other men?"

"That's not true!"

"Indeed it is. But don't let it upset you. How could her going with other men possibly detract from a woman like your wife? You're a handsome couple, you get on well together, you want the same things, you never quarrel, you are well liked by your neighbors . . . The first report from the agency says some very complimentary things about you both: she is twenty-two, teaches at an infant school, is very attractive, lively, and dresses well; he is twenty-seven, an auxiliary teacher at a secondary school, pleasant and of good character; you are very much in love with each other and very close . . . Neither the second nor any of the subsequent reports contradict this as far as you're concerned, but they reveal a wholly unexpected and very surprising side to your wife. The motive is obviously money, which is why, even if you honestly knew nothing about it before, you don't need to worry now. Money, just money . . . Did you know that once, only once, she went to bed with my husband?"

"I suspected it. That is, in the beginning I suspected something. I had believed that the reason your husband became so friendly with us was that he had his eye on my wife. She didn't seem interested, however. And then I stopped being suspicious: I had no reason to think he was after my wife once he had explained what he wanted of us, or rather of me."

"In terms of my husband's plan, however, a little affair with your wife was necessary. He was guarding, I believe, against the possibility that you might betray him either by chance or negligence. Then he could have said that, as a result of your having discovered his affair with your wife, you had killed his in revenge; or that you, having come here to kill him, had met with resistance or some form of aggravation from me that had roused you to violence . . . But you needn't worry that my husband would have deliberately put the police on to you in collusion with your wife: that kind of subtlety is beyond him. And I'm convinced that your wife would never have been party to any such deal: I think I understand the kind of woman she is."

"What kind of woman?"

"She's like me. And many others . . . We worship material things, we have put them in the place of God in our universe of love. Shop windows are our firmament, built-in wardrobes and fitted kitchens contain our world; kitchens not for cooking, inhabited by the gods of the television quiz-games . . . My father, who was *petit-bourgeois*, lived in rented apartments all his life and never felt the need to own his own home. Today there's not a Marxist who doesn't want to own property, who won't saddle himself with debts for the sake of buying his own home. The concepts of eternity and of hell have shrunk to the dimensions of the mortgage repayable over twenty-five years. It's the banks that dispense metaphysics . . . But enough of that . . . Your wife, as I was saying, is like me. We're all alike nowadays, that's the trouble. But your wife is either indifferent or naïve as well. I'm certain that it was she who first leapt at my husband's proposition . . . By the way, what terms did he propose?"

"He has already deposited a large sum of money, in both our names, at a bank in Hamburg."

"How much?"

"Two hundred thousand Deutschmarks."

"So, instead of coming here this evening, you could have taken a plane to Hamburg and . . ."

"I could. But in two years' time, had all gone according to plan, I should have received a further four hundred thousand Deutschmarks."

"From me you will receive five hundred thousand, and after only six months. Do you trust me?"

"I don't know."

"You have to. And remember that where my plan is concerned the risk is minimal, whereas had you gone ahead with the other you would have gone to prison with a certainty that I might well call mathematical. The investigating agency has been instructed, in the eventuality of anything happening to me, to send copies of their reports and photographs to the police . . . But even if I broke my word or was actually planning to put the police on to you, the only risk you run is that of receiving no more money and of being accused of a *crime passionnel* in defense of your honor. You'd get two or three years at most and there's always the chance of a pardon. Indeed, it is imperative that you remember this: if by any chance you are found out, stress your wife's infidelity and the terrible injury that my husband inflicted upon you. Stress it constantly."

"The more I think about it, the more likely it seems that you could be setting a trap for me."

"I would think you an idiot if you went away from here without some such suspicion..." She glanced at the time, rose and asked him with a smile: "Would it be indiscreet if I asked you what you were going to use to kill me?"

"Pistol."

"Excellent... You should go now; if you wait any longer you will be late for your appointment. And good luck."

Smiling sweetly and maternally, she saw him to the door; but before closing it, when he was already nearly at the gate, she recalled him with a whisper. "I advise you to use more than one shot: he's very strong." The advice was given in a tone of solicitude, as if to a sickly child. Then she asked: "You have a silencer, I imagine?"

"On the pistol, yes, I have."

"Good. And, again, good luck!" She shut the door and leaned her shoulders against it. Her smile was one of pure joy as she said, savoring every syllable: "A silencer: premeditated murder." She went to the window and watched him go out through the gate.

She sat down in an armchair; got up; walked around the room; ran her fingers over the furniture and ornaments as if she were playing the piano; stood gazing at the pictures; looked at the clock. Eventually she went to the telephone, dialed a number and asked in a troubled voice: "Is my husband still in the office? . . . He's already gone? . . . I'm worried, terribly worried . . . Yes, I know it's not the first time that he's been late, but something has happened this evening to make me anxious . . . A young man came here to see him; his manner was agitated, menacing; he waited here for some time and has only just left. He frightened me . . . No, I'm sure I'm not imagining things, because I know what is probably behind it . . . How long ago did my husband leave? . . . Yes, thank you. Goodbye . . . Yes, goodbye." She hung up, dialed another number and spoke with even greater anxiety than before, with distress in her tone. "Is that the police station? Is Inspector Scoto there? . . . May I speak to him at once, please? . . . Oh, Inspector, I'm so glad to have caught you in your office at this hour . . . This is Signora Arduini . . . I'm worried, dreadfully worried . . . My husband . . . This is embarrassing and humiliating for me, but I have no choice . . . My husband is having an affair with a married woman; she's very young and extremely attractive . . . I know this is so, because I have had him followed by private detectives, and I'm not ashamed to admit it . . . No, I don't want to accuse him of adultery; on the contrary, I'm worried lest something should have happened to him . . . You see, the woman's husband came here this evening. He's a teacher of mathematics. He seemed extremely agitated and upset. Stupidly, I let him in, and he sat down and waited for my husband; there was something threatening about him. He was here for a couple of hours. I tried to get him to talk but he was curt and evasive. He's gone now . . . Yes, just a few minutes ago. I phoned my husband's office to try and warn him, but he had already left. He should have been home by now. Is there anything you can do? . . . Yes, very well,"— almost in tears—"I'll wait for half an hour and call you again . . . Thank you so much."

A MATTER OF CONSCIENCE

TRAVELING BACK FROM Rome to Maddà, by the train that left at eight in the morning and arrived at seven minutes past midnight, Avvocato Vaccagnino invariably passed the time in a systematic perusal of one daily paper, three "pulp" magazines and a detective novel. He had to make this trip at least once a month; the outward journey was spent in revising and reorganizing the documents that constituted the reason for his trip, while on the return journey he was able to indulge in a rather lighter form of reading matter.

The newspaper, the three magazines and the detective novel were, however, calculated to a nicety to occupy the time of the scheduled journey, the hours between eight and midnight, less the time taken for two meals, one on the train and the other on the ferry, and if the train ran late the lawyer was in trouble: his reading matter exhausted and unable even to look out of the window at the countryside and the sea, now swallowed in amorphous darkness, he would feel an insidious drowsiness creeping up on him to which he dared not succumb for fear of a repetition of the occasion when he had been carried, deeply asleep, to the end of the line. So, as soon as he realized that the train was running behind schedule, Vaccagnino would search the train, almost empty by now, for papers discarded by other travelers. When he had managed to collect a few, no matter whether they were Fascist pamphlets, women's magazines or books of comic strips, he felt safe again.

Thus, one summer night when the train was already forty minutes late at Catania and clearly destined to be a full hour and twenty minutes behind schedule before it arrived at Maddà, Avvocato Vaccagnino found himself immersed in a copy of *Voi*, a weekly magazine for women with features on fashion, the home and topics of the hour. At first he leafed through it, pausing over the photographs of current fashion that, despite covering so small a proportion of the models' flesh, was certainly lively and attractive though just as certainly unsuitable for dressing one's own wife, daughter or sister with any decency. Not that the lawyer himself, for goodness' sake, was so narrow-minded that he would disapprove of modern trends of fashion appearing even in Maddà, but the fact remained that not everyone in Maddà was capable of contemplating the female form as he did, from a purely aesthetic point of view, and if a woman were to walk down the street dressed like that (very low neckline, very brief skirt) she would provoke such a salvo of wolf-whistles and obscene remarks that her husband or father or brother would find himself either obliged to endure it, which would do him no credit at all, or have recourse to violence.

Luckily, the magazine was a thick one. When he reached the last page the lawyer turned back to the beginning to read the articles. There were pages and pages of advertisements, then a column headed: *The Conscience and the Spirit: Father Lucchesini replies to your letters.* Vaccagnino took off his shoes, stretched his legs out on the seat opposite and began to read. Immediately he gave a start of surprise. "A matter of considerable delicacy and complexity has been raised by a reader living in Maddà: 'A few years ago, in a moment of weakness, I was unfaithful to my husband with a man who was a frequent guest at our house, a relative with whom I had been a little bit in love since before my marriage. The affair lasted about six months, but even while it lasted I continued to love my husband; I now love him more than ever before, and the "crush" that I had on my relative is completely over and done with. But I am tormented by the thought of having deceived my husband, a good, loyal and faithful man, and very much in love with me. There are moments when I long to tell him everything, but I hold back for fear of losing him. As a very devout person, I have confessed my fault on several different occasions. Every priest except one (but he was a northerner) has told me that if my repentance is sincere and my love for my husband unchanged, then I must remain silent. But I continue to be tormented. What would you, Father, advise me to do?' "

The jubilation that surged within the lawyer's breast was so intense that it bordered on ecstasy. This letter would provide a topic of conversation for at least a month at the club, among colleagues at the courthouse and within domestic circles. Theories by the hundred would be formulated, numberless private lives —of wives, husbands, wives' relatives—would be put under the microscope and examined with the keenest curiosity; in some cases, like his own, this curiosity would be detached, almost academic; in others it would be malicious, dedicated to the winkling out of every shred of scandal.

He half-closed his eyes and tilted his head back as if seeking illumination from the electric light for the review of suspects that he now began to make, but slowly, like removing the petals of a rose one by one. "Who could it be?" he murmured softly, "Whoever could it be?" Yet he hesitated to concentrate fully on the problem for fear that the identity of the woman, about whom so much could be divined from the letter, should suggest itself too quickly.

And the hesitation was so delicious that it began to induce a delicious drowsiness; he shook it off, however, when it occurred to him that he still hadn't read Father Lucchesini's reply.

The reverend father opened his reply with a rare old burst of righteous indignation: "A moment of weakness? A moment that lasted six months? How can you be so complaisant towards yourself and towards your fault that you can call an infidelity that lasted six months 'a moment of weakness'? SIX MONTHS' betrayal of a man whom you yourself describe as 'good, loyal, faithful and loving'!" After a "but," the priest continued in a gentler, more charitable vein: "But if you have truly repented, if your remorse is sincere and you are determined that never again will you yield to such weakness . . ."— concluding—"You have atoned and continue to atone for your sin with the pangs of remorse; but you cannot and must not allow yourself to confess to a good man, happy in his ignorance, a man who trusts you with the trustingness of true love. To burden him with such knowledge might well cause irreparable damage. Objectively speaking, the impulse to confess to the person one has wronged is in itself admirable; but if the person wronged is oblivious of the fact, then such a revelation can only result in misery and pain and you have a duty to remain silent. Suffer in silence. The priests who advised you to say nothing to your husband were therefore right. With regard to the one who so rashly advised the contrary, I would attribute such advice to a lack of knowledge of the human heart, rather than his being, as you say, a 'northerner.' Pray and keep on praying; and accept reticence as a greater sacrifice than the acknowledgment of your guilt to the man you betrayed."

"What a good reply," thought the lawyer. "An excellent reply. There's indignation, charitableness, common sense: the lot. Must be one of the best, this Father Lucchesini." He gave a big yawn, lit a cigarette and indulged in a daydream where he was surrounded by all the prettiest young ladies of Maddà waiting nervously for a man like him, of high principles and rapier intelligence, to discover which was the guilty one, the adulteress among them.

Refreshed by eight hours of sleep and a large cup of coffee, Avvocato Vaccagnino's thoughts turned again to the letter while he was dressing. He had cut it out and put it away carefully in his wallet although he knew that his wife subscribed to *Voi* and that there must be at least fifty copies around the town. And perhaps this would be as good a starting point as any for an investigation: to list the married women who subscribed to the magazine or who bought it regularly from the newsagent. Nothing could be easier: the owner of the paper-shop was his client, and a word in the ear of the postmaster would send that worthy man hurrying, even at night, to open the sacks of mail. And anyway, with luck he could cull some useful information from his wife. He called her.

When she appeared, with an impatient "What is it?" on her lips, her head bristling with rollers and her face smothered in cream, he suddenly found himself disposed to adopt a disparaging and inquisitorial tone.

"Do you actually read the magazines you buy?"

"Which ones?"

"The women's magazines."

"I only subscribe to *Voi*."

"And you buy the others from the newsagent's."

"Not true. I borrow the others from my friends," said his wife defensively, anticipating yet another lecture about household expenses and the wastefulness and rash purchases which, according to her husband, were all chickens that would come home to roost sooner or later.

But the lawyer had no desire to get bogged down in an argument about the domestic budget. "*Voi*," he said, "You read *Voi*, do you?"

"Of course I read it."

"Do you read Father Lucchesini's column?"

"Sometimes."

"Have you read it this week?"

"No, I haven't. Why?"

"Read it."

"Why?"

"Read it and you'll see."

She hesitated for a moment, wondering whether to

insist upon his telling her what it was that was so interesting, to repay the insult of his tone by the corresponding insult of refusing to read the article, or yield to her own curiosity and rush to read it. Curiosity prevailed, naturally, but she had no intention of giving her husband the satisfaction of revealing her interest in what he had read. So the lawyer, who had hoped to glean some information, some hint of a suspicion from observing her reaction, waited for fifteen minutes and then called her again.

But his wife's voice answered him from behind the locked door of the bathroom, shrill with exasperation: "What's the matter?"

From outside the door he asked, "Have you read it?"

"No," his wife replied curtly.

"Silly cow," said the lawyer, knowing full well that she had read it, but that one of those whims that spiced their marital bliss with variety was dictating that he was to be deprived of the pleasure of discussing it with her.

He had greater luck in the corridors of the courthouse, and the success that he notched up at the club was positively resounding. In the courthouse, the fact that Avvocato Lanzarotta, who carried his fifty years well but had a wife of twenty-five, removed his gown and requested an adjournment of the case in which he was about to appear on the grounds of a sudden indisposition ten minutes after reading the letter, was interpreted correctly by everyone; as was the kind of rigor mortis that was seen to come over Judge Rivera as he scanned the letter line by line before handing it back and returning to his office like a sleepwalker.

The reactions of Lanzarotta and Rivera were duly reported at the club where, with many a compassionate grin, they all agreed that the two must have cause for disquiet. But Don Luigi Amarú, a bachelor, unfeelingly declared that it would be easy to find at least twenty men in the same circumstances as Lanzarotta and Rivera, and without looking further than the circle of one's own friends and acquaintances. "What circumstances?" he was asked by several voices at once. Don Luigi obliged with an analysis: a wife aged between twenty and thirty-five, not unattractive, well educated as one could tell from the letter, with a relative in his forties, good-looking and with some charm, who had been and probably still was a friend of the family, the husband a good man with a calm temperament, not overly intelligent. The unanimous acceptance of this analysis was immediately succeeded by widespread consternation. Leaving aside the question of intelligence, for no one doubted his own standing on that score, there were no fewer than nine men present (someone had already counted) who fitted the description.

Among these, the first to react was Favara, a surveyor. "Let me see that letter again," he said darkly, advancing upon Vaccagnini with a dangerous light in his eyes. The lawyer handed over the slip of paper and Favara, sinking into an armchair, became absorbed in his reading, lavishing upon it the concentration he usually devoted to riddles, brain-teasers and crossword puzzles and oblivious of the silence surrounding him and of the attention, both amused and anxious, of which he had become the focus. Amused, because the bachelors, the widowers, the old men and those fortunate enough to have a wife without relatives, could afford to feel highly entertained; anxious, because those who fulfilled Don Luigi's conditions were now seriously alarmed and were studying Favara's reactions minutely as if he were offering a kind of sacrifice on their behalf which, once accomplished, would restore their shattered sense of security.

In fact, when Favara raised eyes like those of a drowning man from the piece of paper, his reaction was all that could be desired both by those who were sharing his agony and those who were enjoying themselves. "So what are you staring at? Silly, made-up stories . . . I've never believed in letters written to magazines; the journalists write them themselves."

Most of them agreed: "Quite true, he's absolutely right." And they still smiled compassionately.

But Doctor Militello, a man noted for his devoutness and a widower for at least thirty years, objected: "Oh no, my friend. I'll allow that newspapers do fabricate letters of a provocative nature, but here we are dealing with a column written by a priest; and the suggestion that a priest would fabricate anything, let alone in a matter of conscience, I must refute as irreverent and offensive."

"You refute it, do you?" Favara said, his sarcasm a thin cover for the violence seething within him. "And who are you to refute it?"

"What do you mean, who am I?" spluttered the doctor, casting about for an identity that would give him a clear right to crush Favara's insinuation. "You ask me who I am? . . . And who am I?" he asked, turning to the others.

Nicasio, a teacher and the president of the Association of Catholic Teachers, came promptly to the doctor's aid: "He's a Catholic and therefore justified in . . ."

"Whited sepulchres!" shouted Favara, leaping up from his chair. And, preempting the reactions of those he had insulted, he screwed the paper into a ball and hurled it at the piano with such force and fury that it seemed about to transform itself on impact into a cannonball like those displayed at Castel Sant'Angelo; and stormed out.

Silence fell; but a volatile silence that trembled with suppressed mirth. After a moment, Doctor Militello said: "I didn't realize that Favara's wife had any relatives," thus initiating a conversation so intriguing that it was only brought to an end by the appearance of the steward coming to remind them, with the greatest respect, of the time: it was two o'clock.

Avvocato Vaccagnino found his spaghetti overdone and his wife sulking. He ate without complaint, as the fault was his, and attempted to amuse his wife by an account, suitably colored, of the incidents concerning Lanzarotta, Rivera and—last but by no means least—Favara.

But his wife did not seem to appreciate the spirited account.

"What a fine conscience you've got!" she said. "And what if something dreadful should happen?"

"Why on earth should anything dreadful happen?" exclaimed the lawyer. "And even if it did, my conscience is perfectly clear. Firstly, because the letter was published in a magazine read by every rag, tag and bobtail . . ."

"You've read it yourself," observed his wife.

"Only by chance," the lawyer pointed out.

"So because I read it regularly, I am to be included in the general category of 'rag, tag and bobtail'!" The signora, for reasons best known to herself, was spoiling for a fight.

But her husband had no intention of rising to the bait. He apologized and then continued: "Secondly, because no one, absolutely no one, has made any allusions to the private lives of any one of the three: *a*) because there has never been, as far as I know, any gossip concerning the wives of Lanzarotta, Rivera or Favara; *b*) even if there had been, we are all gentlemen and I, perhaps, to an excessive degree; *c*) if a man wishes to advertise the fact that he is a cuckold he is as much at liberty to do so as I am to find it amusing . . ."

"That's just it," interposed his wife. "You find it amusing."

Annoyed at being interrupted in the full spate of enumerating subheadings, at which he was past master, the lawyer raised his voice. "Yes, you're right, I do find it amusing . . . And if you know of any circumstance which should interfere with my right to be amused, you have only to tell me so." And there was already a savage gleam in his eye.

"You bastard!" said his wife, and ran to lock herself in the bedroom.

The lawyer regretted his last remark immediately, but more for its jarring effect upon his own peace of mind than because it had offended his wife. The remark had resurrected the memory of an old tale, and from this old tale there now burgeoned a whole clutch of anxieties, doubts and apprehensions. The tale related how William the Norman commanded that all the cuckolds in his kingdom should wear pointed hoods to distinguish themselves from other men, the penalty for disobedience being one hundred florins. And one particularly law-abiding husband asked his wife to tell him, in all good conscience, if he should or should not wear the pointed hood, arousing the most emphatic protests from her and declarations that no woman alive was more respectful than she of her husband's honor. But when the husband, thus encouraged, was about to leave the house bareheaded, she called him back saying well why not, perhaps, just to be on the safe side, it would be better to wear the hood . . .

"And how can a husband ever be sure?" the lawyer thought; and all that he had ever read about female duplicity and the devilish ingenuity employed by women intent upon adultery, passed before his mind and augmented the sense of self-pity to which he now abandoned himself with all the desperation of a blind man (the comparison leapt to his mind) lamenting his disability. And he really did feel himself to be in a state of physical blindness, blundering about in the total obscurity that concealed the whole of his wife's existence before he had married her, the hours she spent alone, the freedom she enjoyed, her real feelings, her real thoughts. "One has to be philosophical," he reflected; and found his philosophy in a mental image of Marcus Aurelius towering immobile above the sinuous, erotic nudity of Messalina. Heaven knows where the idea had come from, but he had a rooted conviction that Messalina had been the wife of Marcus Aurelius and that the latter had become a philosopher in order to cope with his marital problems.

Philosophy permeated the club that evening. Judge Rivera and the lawyer Lanzarotta were both present, pretending (as one could tell from the pallor of their faces and the nervous shiftiness of their eyes) to a calm indifference. Many others were attempting to suppress uneasiness, anxiety and fear, including Avvocato Vaccagnino, despite the fact that he was fortunate enough—in the eyes of his friends at least—to number among his wife's relatives only one cousin who lived in Detroit and had never shown up in town, and one aunt who belonged to an enclosed order of nuns.

Favara had done all he could to put everyone's mind at rest, going straight from the club to subject his wife to an exhaustive interrogation even to the point (so it was whispered) of having recourse to physical persuasion; and because his wife denied, desperately and emphatically denied, ever having been guilty of such a fault and of having written the letter, Favara had decided that there was only one thing to be done: to rush to Milan, find Father Lucchesini and persuade him to show him the letter. And, just in case Father Lucchesini should be difficult to persuade, he had put a revolver in his pocket. So as soon as he had left the house, his wife phoned his partner Basicò and begged him, out of loyalty to his friend and colleague, to rescue him from the impending disaster; and Basicò, who was a true friend, rushed to Catania airport, calculating that Favara, who was traveling by train (fact confirmed by the station master) would arrive in Milan the following morning. But the fact that he was a friend hadn't stopped him informing Doctor Militello, and therefore the entire membership of the club, of the delicate and secret mission upon which he was embarking.

Everyone, therefore, was now busily applying philosophy to Favara's case, declaring the suspicions that had maddened him to be unfounded—though privately hoping against hope that they would prove to be extremely well founded. They even decided that the letter must have been written by some mischief-maker in Maddà with the express intention of provoking just this situation; for there was certainly no lady in Maddà who would have been capable of anything so rash and foolish.

"If I find out who did it," said the teacher Cozzo, "I'll wring his neck, by God I will!"

As Cozzo was a bachelor, they were all surprised at such vehemence, and someone asked, "Surely it doesn't concern you that much?"

"I know whether it concerns me or not," said Cozzo, thumping his right fist angrily into the palm of his left hand.

And it did in fact concern him materially. He had had an appointment, the first, with Nicasio's wife in a hotel in the big town nearby; but the lady had canceled it saying that it was absolutely impossible, on this day of all days, to tell her husband that she was going into town alone to do the shopping; her husband had been difficult to talk to at lunch, all bad temper and suspicion.

Cozzo's attitude gave rise to a new wave of speculation, though this remained secret and under the surface. To Nicasio, who was also there at the time, it brought back memories of the carnival ball at which his wife had danced nearly the whole evening with Cozzo (and they had quarreled about it later at home).

All in all, it was a long evening for many; but for others it was all too short.

Avvocato Zarbo went to bed before his wife as usual. His day had been a bad one, on account of the letter. In court, at the club and above all within himself, he had struggled with the conflicting emotions of anger and pity, love and rancor. Not like the others. He knew, he had always known.

He picked up his book and opened it where he had left off the night before. He read a few pages, but a shutter seemed to have descended between his eyes and his brain and his mind was in a state of miserable confusion. Looking up from his book, he was almost startled by the sight of his wife standing naked, her arms in the air, her head hidden by the nightdress she was in the act of putting on. It seemed the right moment, and he asked her, keeping his voice level and toneless: "Why did you write that letter to Father Lucchesini?"

Her head emerged from the nightdress as if it had been wrenched out, her face frozen in a grimace of bewilderment and fear. She almost shouted: "Who told you?"

"Nobody. I realized immediately that the letter was yours."

"Why? How?"

"Because I knew."

She fell to her knees and buried her face against the edge of the bed as if to suffocate the cry: "So you knew! You knew!" And she stayed there, shaken by silent sobs.

He began to speak of his love and his grief, looking at her with tenderness mingled with contempt, pity mingled with desire and shame. And when his voice became choked with tears and he began to weep, he reached out his arms to raise her up and draw her to him.

But as soon as he touched her she sprang to her feet and began to laugh a malicious laughter that left her mouth and her eyes cold and immobile. She held out her clenched fist towards him, flicked out her index and fourth finger as if to gouge out his eyes, and from her throat came, hysterical and harrowing, the bleating of a goat. "Beeeee . . . Beeeee . . ."

APOCRYPHAL CORRESPONDENCE
RE CROWLEY

To the Chief of Police
Institute enquiries into the activities of British subject
Edward Alexander Crowley in Cefalù and report.

M.

To His Excellency Benito Mussolini
Prime Minister

ROME, 15 JULY 1924

With reference to the memorandum from Your Excellency requesting enquiries into the activities of the
English national E. A. Crowley currently resident in
Cefalù (Palermo), I append a summary of the report just
received from the Commissariat of Public Security in that
locality.

"The subject of this report, Edward Alexander Crowley, (also known as Aleister Crowley), was born in Leamington on 12 October 1875 and has been occupying a villa situated about 3 km outside the town since April 1920. He is punctual in the payment of his rent and the only complaint that the proprietors have is that Crowley has a mania for painting frescoes, suspected of being indecent, on the internal walls of the villa; the proprietors have, however, been unable to inspect the villa for themselves since renting it to Crowley and have only heard of the Englishman's strange obsession from the rumors circulating in the town, which rumors are enhanced by the fact that Crowley lives with no less than five women, all relatively young and attractive (as well as three children of whom one is black or of mixed race) about whom the local imagination, predictably in a community such as this, has built so many strange and exotic fantasies that it is no longer possible to separate truth from fiction. It would seem, however, that the eccentricities of which the villagers accuse Crowley can all be attributed solely to a back-to-nature style of life, evidenced by the children, the women and Crowley himself having been observed to indulge in nude sunbathing, though no complaints about this have been submitted to this commissariat. On the contrary, the villagers seem to spend a good deal of their time spying upon the villa (which, it should be noted, is well shielded from public view) and the nudity of the young women has occasioned so much pleasurable interest that the resultant gossip has achieved scandalous proportions. We were informed of this by His Excellency the Lord Bishop, but our own discreet enquiries revealed nothing apart from an encroachment on the part of the local residents upon the individual's right to privacy, a right accorded to every citizen and which the English, in particular, hold dear. We have therefore decided to take no further action, beyond assuring His Excellency the Lord Bishop that we would keep the villa under observation and that should its inhabitants be found infringing any of the laws of our country, we should take immediate and positive steps.

"To summarize: Crowley's way of life is indubitably different from that of most people, but it is mysterious rather than scandalous; and it is this mystery which makes Crowley's presence in Cefalù a cause of local unease. As regards the possibility of his being a spy or indulging in any activity to the detriment of State security, we believe any such suspicion to be entirely unfounded. Suffice it to say that his connections with the outside world are limited to the provisioning of the villa, which is usually accomplished by one visit a month to a local shop. From this and from our knowledge that the villa is provided with its own wood-fired oven, we have deduced that the women bake all the bread that is required, while their meat (if they eat meat) is obtained from the slaughter of the goats and other farmyard animals that they rear themselves."

If I can be of any further service, I shall be happy to oblige. With Fascist greetings,

Gen. E. De Bono
Chief of Police

Memo to the Chief of Police
Investigation of English national Crowley must be continued. Make an on-the-spot check. Report back. Who said he was suspected of spying? It's the British Ambassador who's worried: anxious lest any scandal surrounding his compatriot should damage the reputation of his country. I couldn't care less.

M.

To His Excellency Benito Mussolini
Prime Minister

ROME, 11 SEPTEMBER 1924

In response to the instructions received from Your Excellency with regard to the English national Edward Alexander Crowley (also known as Aleister Crowley), currently resident in Cefalù (Palermo), I enclose the report from the Commissioner of the local branch of the Office of Public Security. With Fascist greetings,

Gen. E. De Bono
Chief of Police

To His Excellency the Chief of Police

ROME

In response to the instructions contained in Your Excellency's letter of 20 July 1924, Ref. 19328, the undersigned has applied himself with the greatest diligence to this very sensitive undertaking. In the first instance, to preempt any misunderstanding on the part of the local judiciary, he informed the Public Prosecutor in Cefalù as to the instructions received, thereby ensuring that the search of the villa conformed to the requirements of the law and that in the case of the Englishman complaining about invasion of privacy, we should not be faced with the subsequent displeasure of the Prosecutor as well. In spite of the elevated provenance of the instructions and of the possibility that the interests of the State might be involved, the requested permission was not accorded without hesitation or delay, hence the time-lapse in my delivering this report to Your Excellency based on information which I was able, eventually, to gather personally.

The search of the Crowley villa was conducted by the undersigned with the assistance of Brigadier Angelo Lo Turco and Agent Bartolomeo Vasta during the forenoon of the 7th inst., accompanied by Professore Paolo D'Alunzio, teacher of English at the local Technical College whom the undersigned invited to act as interpreter should this be required. In the event, it was found unnecessary to have recourse to the services of an interpreter, since

161

Crowley's command of Italian is sufficient to be comprehensible. The presence of the teacher was, however, useful for the clarification of one small detail, as will appear later.

To begin with, Crowley evinced indignation at the fact that an individual, violating no law and giving no cause for public disapprobation, should be subjected in Italy to an investigation in patent opposition to the principle of individual liberty; but he very soon adopted an attitude of condescension and even of amusement, assuming a role like that of a museum guide, not without a preliminary explanation of the philosophy by which he and the others live and to which their surroundings testify. This philosophy, if the undersigned may be permitted to have recourse to memories of his own grammar school studies, would seem to be an admixture of certain elements such as magic and astrology from the ancient civilizations of the Middle East with elements of a watered-down Epicureanism in the widely accepted sense, defined by Horace as *epicure grege porcum*, and, in complete contrast, a streak of savage pessimism. The whole is sublimated in a ritual that has been borrowed partly from the Catholic Church and partly from Freemasonry, to judge from the implements used in this ritual and which were shown to us and explained. Chains and instruments for flagellation were naturally present, for according to this religion which Crowley claims to have founded, a religion of sun and blood, pleasure cannot be achieved without first experiencing pain. By this is probably implied the pain of others, though Professore D'Alunzio assures me that practices of reciprocal or self-flagellation are methods commonly used in England for the procurement of pleasure.

The undersigned can now confirm from his own observation the reports concerning the frescoes painted by Crowley on the internal walls of the villa. The paintings depict, not unskillfully, strange positions for intercourse and also scenes of depravity including sodomy; and everywhere are displayed, like recurring ornamental *motifs*, those parts of the human anatomy which common decency requires should be concealed and never mentioned. Crowley attempted to convince the undersigned that the entire content and meaning of life consists solely in that which is portrayed and practiced by himself; that man's every thought and action stems from this and, though in a wide variety of guises, fulfills it. He then went on to express his enthusiasm for the Fascist movement and its leader, and declared himself happy to be a guest in a country such as Italy, where, thanks to Fascism, the ideals now tallied so closely with his own. The undersigned felt it his duty to repudiate this particular compliment, but Crowley was very insistent, putting forward arguments that, although contorted and specious, yet did not lack intelligence. Later, upon the undersigned's remarking a square-shaped stone which bore traces of bloodstains, and inquiring as to its use, Crowley replied that this was the place of sacrifice; but he added an aside in English of which the undersigned caught only the name Matteotti. Professore D'Alunzio translated Crowley's words verbatim as: "The honorable Matteotti was killed elsewhere." This was probably ironic.

As far as the women are concerned, although it must be presumed that they live in a state of slavery, they neither appear unhappy nor do they complain of their lot.

At the time of our visit to the villa, the children were asleep beneath a tree. They appear to be in the best of health.

To conclude, the impressions received by the undersigned were totally unfavorable and would provide ample grounds for expelling Crowley from Italy; this view is reinforced by the evidence of villagers to the effect that on more than one occasion, one or another of Crowley's women has been seen tied naked to a rock and exposed to the full force of the sun throughout the hottest part of the day.

Please let me know if I can be of any further service.

With Fascist greetings,

A. Caminiti

Commissioner

CEFALÙ, 8 SEPTEMBER 1924

To the Chief of Police

Take urgent steps for the expulsion of Mr. Crowley from Italy. The Cefalù Commissioner is an idiot.

M.

To the Minister for Foreign Affairs

Inform the British Ambassador that the Minister of the Interior has decided to expel Mr. Crowley from Italy.

M.

MAFIA WESTERN

A BIG TOWN, almost the size of a city, on the border between the provinces of Palermo and Trapani. The First World War is in progress. And, as if that were not enough, there is another, internal one being waged: no less bloody, with a death-toll from assassination comparable to the death-toll of its citizens falling at the Front. Two Mafia cells are engaged in a long-standing feud. A monthly average of two deaths. And every time, everyone knows whose hand was on the trigger and who will answer for it with his life. Even the carabinieri know. It's almost a game, played by the rules of a game. Young *mafiosi* avid for promotion on the one side, old *mafiosi* defending their positions on the other. The death of a henchman from one faction is followed by the death of a henchman from the other. The leaders are unruffled:

they are awaiting negotiations. Possibly, when peace has been restored, one of the leaders, the old one or the young one, will die in the internecine maelstrom of friendship.

But now something strange happens: the feud intensifies, involving ever higher ranks in the hierarchy. In the normal course of events, this is a sign that the side promoting the violence wants peace. This is the moment when the patriarchs bestir themselves from their neighboring villages and come into town to interview both factions, to unite them, to convince the young ones that they can't have everything and the old ones that they can't keep it all to themselves. There is an armistice, a treaty. And, when the reunification has been accomplished, one of the leaders will be eliminated by emigration, superannuation or death. But this time is different. The patriarchs arrive, delegations of the two factions meet, but meanwhile, contrary to custom and expectation, the rhythm of the executions continues unabated, becomes, indeed, even more frenetic, more implacable. Each faction, in the presence of the patriarchs, accuses the other of treachery. The town can make neither head nor tail of what is happening. Nor can the carabinieri. By great good fortune, the patriarchs are men of cool, clear judgment. They bring the two delegations together again, present them with a list of all those who have been assassinated over the past six months and from the resultant dialogue—"This one we killed," "This was ours," "This was nothing to do with us," "Nor with us"—arrive at the disconcerting conclusion that two thirds of the deaths can be attributed to neither side and must therefore be the work of an outsider. Can it be that there is a third cell, secret and invisible, dedicated to the extermination of both the quasi-official ones? Or is there some avenger working on his own, a lone wolf, a madman making a hobby of slaying *mafiosi* on both sides? The consternation is great. Even among the carabinieri, who, although they have been collecting the corpses with a certain degree of satisfaction (the bullets having nailed criminals where convictions had failed), have nevertheless got to the point, their hands already full with the problem of deserters, where they would like to see an end to this civic feud.

The patriarchs, having put their finger accurately on the problem, left it up to the two cells to resolve it as quickly as possible. They then made themselves scarce, because in the circumstances, neither of the two factions, nor both acting collectively, was in a position to guarantee them safe conduct. The *mafiosi* of the town began to make their own investigations; but fear, the sense of being the objects of an inscrutable vendetta or homicidal whim, and finding themselves suddenly in exactly the same position in which they themselves had placed honest people for so long, left them bewildered and robbed of much of their will to act. They were reduced to imploring their political members in their turn to implore the carabinieri to mount a real, thorough-going and efficient investigation—even though they suspected that the carabinieri themselves, having failed to smoke them out by legal methods, might have resorted to this shadier, more secure one. After all, if the government could arrange for a cholera epidemic every now and then to solve the problem of overpopulation, why should one not suppose that the carabinieri might adopt this secret method of extermination against the Mafia?

The hunt for the unknown man, or men, goes on. The leader, or *capo*, of the older Mafia faction also falls a victim. There is a sense of liberation throughout the town as well as of alarm. The carabinieri are completely nonplussed. The *mafiosi* are terrified. But immediately after the funeral of the old *capo* (attended by the entire town with a great show of assumed grief), the *mafiosi* cease to give the impression of being bewildered and frightened. The conviction spreads that they know the identity of the assassin and that his days are numbered. A *capo* is a *capo* even in death, and somehow, as the old man lay dying, he managed to convey some hint, to point the finger in some way. And his friends have now succeeded in identifying the assassin. He is a man whom no one would ever have suspected, a professional man of good character and well respected; though of a somewhat taciturn disposition and given to a solitary lifestyle, there is no one in the entire town (apart from the *mafiosi*, who know) who would ever have dreamed that he was capable of conducting that long drawn out, pitiless and deadly vendetta that had already consigned to the autopsy-bench a fair number of those men that the carabinieri had never succeeded in holding for more than a few hours. And the *mafiosi* had also remembered why, after so many years, this man's hatred of them should have issued with such cold and deadly calculation in this series of executions. There was, needless to say, a woman involved.

Since his student days, he had been romantically attached to a girl who came from a doubtfully noble, but certainly wealthy family. After graduating, he approached her family with the confidence inspired by the strength of their mutual feelings, and formally asked for her hand. He was rejected; because he was poor and because his professional future, given the poverty of his origins, was insecure. But he and the girl continued to see each other, and the feeling between them became even more profound by reason of the difficulties that lay ahead. So the noble and wealthy relatives of the girl appealed to the Mafia for assistance. The *capo*, the old and much feared *capo*, summoned the young man and attempted, with much quoting of proverb and precept, to persuade him to give up the girl. When this failed, he had recourse to open threats. The young man shrugged it off, but the impression made upon the girl was dire. Fearing that the terrible threats would be carried out, and perhaps finally convinced that their love was in any case impossible, she hastily married one of her own set. The young man became gloomy and withdrawn but showed no signs of being desperate or even excessively angry. Evidently, he began to plot his revenge from that moment.

Now the Mafia had discovered his identity and he was a marked man. The sentence was to be executed by the son of the dead *capo*: his was the right, by virtue of his bereavement and the rank held by his late father. The habits of the condemned man, the topography of the district in which he lived and that of the house itself, were studied carefully. The point was overlooked, however, that by now everyone had realized that the Mafia knew: their habitual arrogance had returned and their fear of the unknown danger had obviously vanished. And the very first person to realize all this had been the condemned man himself.

The youthful avenger slipped out of his house one night with the viaticum of the maternal blessing, and made his way to the house of the pharmacist, which was quite close by. There he hid himself to await the other man's return; or he tried to enter the house in order to surprise the man as he slept; or he knocked, expecting him to come to this window or to step onto that balcony. All that is certain is that his intended victim had anticipated him and now turned the tables upon him. The widow of the *capo* and mother of the young man heard a shot. Imagining the vendetta safely accomplished, she awaited her son's return with an anxious heart that became even more alarmed as the minutes ticked away. At last, the appalling truth dawned upon her. She went out and found her son lying dead outside the house of the man who, according to all the plans and the promises, should have died that night. She picked up the body, carried it home and laid it upon the bed. The next morning she let it be known that her son had died of a wound there upon his bed, but that she knew neither where nor by whom he had been wounded. No word did she utter to the carabinieri about the man who might have killed him. But her friends understood—they knew—and they now set about very careful preparations.

Towards the end of a summer's day, when the piazza was filled with people enjoying the first cool evening breezes seated outside their clubs, cafés and shops (and the man who had eluded the Mafia's revenge was also there, sitting in front of the chemist's shop), a man tried to start up his car. He swung the starting handle and the engine burst into life with a violent grinding of metal parts and a volley of crackles that sounded like machine-gun fire. When the noise had died away, there, sprawled upon a chair in front of the chemist's shop, his heart pierced by a rifle bullet, lay the body of the man who had succeeded in sowing death and fear among the ranks of one of the most battle-hardened Mafia cells in the whole of Sicily.

TRIAL BY VIOLENCE

ON THE MORNING of 8 December 1870, a holiday in honor of the Feast of the Immaculate Conception, from the Bergamasque village of Bottanuco which then comprised about one thousand souls, one of which was indubitably black, a fourteen-year-old girl set out for the nearby village of Suisio to spend the day with relatives. She worked as a maid in the household of the Ravasio family, from whom she had had permission for the day's leave and to whom she had promised that she would be back the same evening. The girl and her mistress left the house together but soon parted company. This was around, or shortly after, seven o'clock and it was barely light. Given the early hour, the lonely road and the wintry weather, the older woman was conscious of a feeling of vague unease as she watched the girl walk away. A few minutes later, as she took her own way towards Madone, she heard a series of high-pitched screams, the kind of noise made by a wolf; and this, she decided, was the obvious explanation, for, with the snow on the ground, it was more than likely that the wolves would be having a hard time of it. They had never, however, been known to attack people in that region, so the fact that the screams came from the direction in which the girl had disappeared gave her no additional anxiety. She remembered those screams two days later, on the evening of the 10th, for the girl had not returned on the evening of the 8th, nor the following day, and had never reached Suisio.

They found her in an open-fronted cattle shelter. "The unfortunate girl was lying on the ground, completely naked apart from a stocking on her left leg; her body bore traces of an extraordinarily vicious assault. Disfigured by many wounds, it had been almost completely cleft in two and some parts, notably the intestines, were missing. These were found in the hollow of a tree. And in a thatched hut nearby were found a piece of her left calf and a medallion bearing a portrait of Pope Pius IX, the property of the dead girl. Her clothes were found beneath a pile of maize-stalks at a neighboring farm and her kerchief in the road, lying in the snow. Finally, it was observed that, near the body, arranged in a strangely symmetrical pattern, lay the ten long pins that the girl used to wear in her hair." (This, and some of the other details that were to emerge in later reports inspire a comparison between the unfortunate Giovannina Motta setting out from the house and Lucia, heroine of Manzoni's *I promessi sposi* preparing for her wedding: "The black, girlish hair, parted in the middle with a delicate white line, was gathered at the back of the head into several rings of plaits secured by long silver pins that formed a halo-like effect; a fashion still observed by Milanese women of today. Around her neck she wore a dainty necklace of garnets . . ." But Giovannina's necklace was of small coral beads.)

The hairpins had been laid out in a fan-like pattern. The assassin had maybe tried to reproduce their arrangement in the girl's hair or to imitate the rays of a monstrance. There was not a single spot of blood on the clothes, indicating that the girl must have been stripped before she was killed. A fractured right elbow, scratches on the legs and the presence of soil in the mouth all suggested that the girl had put up a fight and that she had screamed.

The first suspect was a builder from Suisio, one Abramo Esposito, who was arrested. The name suggests one of Southern Italian origin. Was that the reason he was arrested, because he came from the South? But he had nothing whatever to do with the crime and his alibi was solid anyway. He was freed "immediately"; though, having to wait upon the decision of the court in Bergamo, "immediately" meant after a couple of months in prison. With Esposito free, the investigation had no lead and no suspect. But, in the village, the memory of that hideous crime and anxiety about the dangerous criminal still at large, lingered on. Thus it was, that when his wife had been absent for barely two hours, from six until eight, on the morning of Sunday, 27 August 1871, Antonio Frigeni began to search for her most anxiously. He found her quite near the place to which she had told him she was going, in a maize-field, completely naked and no less mutilated than Giovannina. "There was extensive bruising to the neck where the skin had been indented and lacerated by a length of cord, recovered at the scene of the crime, which had evidently been thrown over her head and then drawn tight in the manner of a lasso, and from which she had attempted to free herself as was obvious from the scratches on either side of the neck. According to the experts' opinion, the resulting strangulation was the sole cause of death. But, after death, no respect had been shown to her remains. A number of large gashes in the abdomen, the right arm, the back of the neck and the arms, had all been inflicted after death with some substantial weapon with a point and a blade, probably a reaping-hook. Through the massive wound in the abdomen, the intestines were spilling out. Three hairpins were found stuck into the woman's back . . ." Hairpins; and arranged to form an exact triangle pointing to the nape of the neck.

As on the first occasion, an immediate arrest was sought. The choice fell upon Luigi Comerio, a villager from Suisio, the grounds for his arrest being that "he had lusted after Elisabetta Frigeni and had attempted to procure an act of infidelity to her marriage vows." But there

was no proof that he had ever lusted after Giovannina
Motta and his alibi was unshakable.

Six months passed, every possible line of enquiry had
been exhausted and both the investigators and the public
had become resigned to the mystery, when suddenly,
through the emergence of some information previously
withheld, one name began to be bandied about: Vincenzo Verzeni. "This man was a youth of twenty-two,
came from a peasant family in comfortable circumstances, had been born in Bottanuco and was still living
there. Until this moment he had been regarded as a young
man of sound principles, much given to religious observance, with no known vices; no one would ever have
thought him capable of such horrendous crimes had it
not been for a series of incidents about which, until this
moment, nothing had ever been heard."

Four years previously, on some feast day or another
(religious feast days and Sundays recur with some regu-
larity in the incidents connected with Verzeni) a twelve-
year-old girl, Maria Verzeni, was assaulted in her bed
while resting or sleeping in the late afternoon. Waking to
find a pillow over her face and a hand around her neck,
she had managed to free herself for long enough to utter
a cry, and the attacker had fled. A woman who lived in
the adjoining house saw Vincenzo Verzeni, the girl's
cousin, steal furtively from his own home into the house
of his relatives and leave it again after a few minutes.
Seconds later she had heard the girl cry out, and she was

absolutely clear on the point that Verzeni had already left the house. According to a rather more coherent version, supplied by the girl's aunt, the cries were heard first, then Verzeni was seen on the steps, leaving the house. Verzeni's own version was that he had heard the girl's cries, ran to help her, but finding her naked was constrained by his sense of modesty to leave immediately.

Three years previously, two women had been attacked within a very short space of time as they made their way to the parish church in the early morning. One of them, Barbara Bravi, was seized around the neck but managed to cry out, causing the attacker to flee. Her stronger and more intrepid companion, Margherita Sala, seized their assailant by his shirt and his lower lip, shaking him off after a prolonged struggle and making her escape. Neither of the women recognized the man but certain details of the description they later provided, such as his youthful strength, build, height, jacket of the heavy hairy material known as plush, fitted Verzeni. Moreover, a certain Pozzi remembered that he had actually seen Verzeni upon the very same road on the very same morning, and had noted that he had a scratch upon his left cheek (but not on his lower lip).

During that same month of December, a twelve-year-old girl, Angela Previtali, was accosted by Verzeni while on her way to school (hence it was a weekday, but there was probably some religious observance afoot). With no show of violence, but only a gentle urging, he had taken her by the hand and attempted to lead her towards that same cattle shelter where the mutilated body of Giovannina Motta was later to be discovered. To begin with she had allowed herself to be led a little way, but then screamed and ran off. Verzeni had followed her quite calmly for a little while.

In April 1871, a village woman, Maria Galli, had been accosted by a stranger whom she subsequently identified as Vincenzo Verzeni, who wrested her scarf from her head and ran off with it. On 26 August of the same year, the day before the murder of Elisabetta Frigeni, a nineteen-year-old spinner, Maria Previtali, had been followed and at a certain point accosted by Verzeni whom she "knew well" as he was her cousin. He had managed to throw her to the ground and lift up her skirts, but when she screamed, Verzeni, who had his hand around her neck, released her while he ran to the road to see if there was anyone coming. By the time he returned she was on her feet. He "took both her hands between his own and held them for a time without speaking, then, in response to her pleas, he released her."

To these accounts, so belatedly added to the growing body of evidence, two more were no less belatedly added. The first came from Rosa and Carolina Previtali, who declared that they had seen Verzeni on that fatal 8 December 1870, in the cattle shelter where the crime was committed and after hearing cries for help and groans (though they did not see Giovannina, either alive or dead, nor did the cries alarm them in any way). The second account came from Giovanni Bravi, who said that he had seen Verzeni on 27 August 1871 in the very place where the body of Elisabetta Frigeni was eventually found, and at approximately the time at which she was presumed to have been murdered.

But when the case came to trial, there was an immediate courtroom sensation. Carolina Previtali, asked to state whether the man she saw in the cattle shelter looked like Verzeni or not, answered emphatically in the negative. Reminded that at the judicial enquiry she had said she had recognized him, she denied it. Confronted by her father insisting that she had said the young man looked like Verzeni, she denied this absolutely, repeating: "I said nothing." The Public Prosecutor asked for her arrest and summary trial. The court adjourned, leaving the hall agog and Previtali pleading with his daughter to repeat her identification. When the court reconvened, the girl apologized, declaring herself satisfied that the man she saw in the cattle shelter was indeed "very like Verzeni." And the trial once more got under way.

Verzeni continued to insist upon his innocence. All the evidence against him was purely circumstantial. Of the scraps of direct evidence, the most serious was that contributed by Maria Previtali, yet it fell far short of investing with homicidal intent an incident which she had regarded at the time as an impetuous attempt upon her virtue (ending in that rather pathetic holding of her hands) which only later, after the discovery of the murders and hearing Verzeni accused and execrated as the possible assassin, took on the character of something infinitely more sinister from which she had been lucky to escape.

But the accused had no alibi—except his attendances at Mass. He had attended three on the day of Giovannina Motta's death, three on the day of Elisabetta Frigeni's. And on both those days he had been to confession and taken Communion. But it is interesting to look at some of the exchanges that took place during the examination.

PRESIDENT OF THE TRIBUNAL: When was the last time you saw Giovannina Motta before her death?

DEFENDANT: In October, working in the fields.

PRESIDENT: Have you recently heard anything relating to her?

DEFENDANT: Yes, so have you . . . (*Laughter*)

PRESIDENT: Maybe, but I want to hear about it from you.

DEFENDANT: She was in a terrible mess, *kaput*, you couldn't even tell she was human, she had no clothes on, she was naked . . .

PRESIDENT: Naked?

DEFENDANT: Yes, naked, nothing on at all . . .

PRESIDENT: Was the body itself whole?

DEFENDANT: No, almost split in two, front and back.

PRESIDENT: And the head?

DEFENDANT: I didn't see it.

PRESIDENT: When did you see the body?

DEFENDANT: After early Mass, the day they found her. I was there along with the others.

PRESIDENT: How did you know what had happened?

DEFENDANT: I stayed there . . . Or rather . . . I heard everyone talking about it.

PRESIDENT: And what were they saying?

DEFENDANT: That this was something monstrous, inhuman.

PRESIDENT: It was generally known, was it not, that the girl had gone to Suisio for the festival of Our Lady? And was there not some anxiety about her having failed to return? Do you know, of your own knowledge, how long she had been gone?

DEFENDANT: I didn't hear anything, nor do I know anything, about all that.

PRESIDENT: Did you not know that she had gone on a day's leave?

DEFENDANT: Why should I? It was none of my business.

PRESIDENT: Were you at or near the scene of the murder on the Day of the Immaculate Conception?

DEFENDANT: No.

PRESIDENT: What were your movements on that morning?

DEFENDANT: I went to Mass at six o'clock, then went home; then I went back to the church, made my confession and received Holy Communion. (*Laughter*)

PRESIDENT: And you went nowhere else at all?

DEFENDANT: No. I attended the second, and later High Mass.

PRESIDENT: So you were in church practically the whole time. When you saw Giovannina Motta's body in the cattle shelter, was it covered?

DEFENDANT: It had been covered over. But she was naked...

PRESIDENT: Now we come to the second murder... What were you doing on Sunday, 27 August?

DEFENDANT: I got up in time to go to early Mass, made my confession to Father Martina and received Holy Communion from the parish priest; (*laughter*); I attended the second Mass, celebrated by Father Bartolo, and the third, taken by the curate called Curradù. Then I came away and walked through the fields—others say that I went home...

This last stroke, if not deliberately sly, was certainly sensible, implying: I can really hardly be expected to recall my movements on a particular day three years ago. That I went to the Masses, to confession and Communion, certainly, for I do that every Sunday as a matter of duty; but as for the rest, well, why not accept what the others say, since they seem to remember so much more about my movements than I do myself . . . Indeed, his replies are all judicious, and to the extent that they are judicious, they are imbued with the indifference of a man who recognizes the total impotence of common sense as a weapon against the ridiculous machine of the Law. Verzeni only makes three little slips in his replies to the judge, the first when he says "I stayed there . . ." (where? at the scene of the crime, after committing it?), and the other two when he seems to have been caught in a kind of residual raptus, still gloating irresistibly over the memory or his own imaginary evocation of the victims' nudity. But neither the prosecutor nor any of the tribunal judges was quick enough to spot the slips and turn them to account.

Faced with the contradiction between the "abnormality" of the crimes and the apparent "normality," both physical and mental, of the man to whom they were attributed, the court had a problem of responsibility to resolve. It should be borne in mind that the defense, and the defendant himself, were adducing the following arguments for the purposes of establishing the "normality" of the accused: Verzeni's tireless devotion to religious practices (the continual cycle of Masses, confessions and Communions), the fact that at twenty-two he had had no intimate relations with women nor had ever indulged in solitary erotic practices, and his well-attested aversion to the slaughter of chickens (killed, of course, by having their necks wrung). The wheel has now come full circle, and nowadays no barrister worth his salt would be unaware of the negative value of such evidence, but then such facts as these were part of the defense.

However, in order to tackle the problem scientifically, the court turned for assistance to the man who currently enjoyed the reputation of the greatest criminologist of his time, Professor Cesare Lombroso, founder of the *positive school of penal law.*

Professor Lombroso was naturally unwilling to make any "off the cuff" pronouncement. Firstly, he asked for an expert examination of the defendant's retinas, "since the retina is like a window opening upon the brain." Then he required that the defendant's head should be completely shaved so that a "craniometrical" examination could be made, indispensable for determining the presence of madness or criminal inclinations. On hearing the second request, the prosecutor leapt to his feet with an objection: If the defendant were shaved, how would witnesses be able to identify him? The objection was sustained, and the defendant directed to be shaved *after* the witnesses had made their identification.

Once the professor had him in his hands, it took no more than a week for all the requisite examinations to be carried out. And not only of the defendant himself, for the canons of the "school" required that the examinations should extend to the parents, grandparents, aunts and uncles, and cousins of the accused. The father was found to have slight symptoms of pellagra, two uncles were declared "cretinoid" (one in particular, having an undersized cranium with a markedly conical formation, no growth of beard, one testicle atrophic and the other completely absent), one cousin was discovered to be suffering from cerebral hyperemia and another from kleptomania. His mother, his surviving grandmother, his great-grandparents and great-great-grandparents, were not, however, "suspected of any abnormal disease or disability." All in all, this was the kind of result that could be obtained from an examination of any ordinary family. Note that word "cretinoid," which the professor defined as a less pronounced form of mental malady, "describing one who partakes both of the nature of the cretin and that of the sane person." We might regret that so obviously useful a term should have remained the property of the experts and not descended into everyday parlance, where it would be most welcome as a means of referring to those who commit the actions of a cretin with, apparently, the tools of ratiocination.

According to the professor, Verzeni could not even be properly declared "cretinoid," but only affected by the "slight taint of the cretinous and the pellagrous that runs in his family and which has left traces upon his right frontal lobe and disrupted the balance of the affective faculty in relation to the appetites." However, the professor specifically excluded any possibility of this disturbance, even when exacerbated by the repressive family circumstances and the "prurience of the chaste," causing any lapse of the consciousness and therefore a state of irresponsibility. The most that could be claimed along these lines was that the accused "was entirely responsible when initiating the act, less so during the frenzy of its execution"—and that he returned to a state of full responsibility afterwards while evading capture.

When Professor Lombroso's report had been read out in court, the public prosecutor, Cavalier Quintavalle, launched into his address. First he conjured up an image of each victim as she had appeared in life: Giovannina Motta, "lively, intelligent, blooming with health and vitality, an example to her companions of sobriety and purity of life," and Elisabetta Frigeni, "mother of two tender infants, one not yet weaned." He then described them in death, sparing none of the most gruesome details. He concluded, "All I can do now is to entrench myself behind the opinion of the experts." And entrench himself he did, impregnably.

Verzeni was sentenced to hard labor for life.

EUPHROSYNE

I HAVE READ Stendhal's *Chroniques italiennes* many times, at intervals of years or months, but it was only yesterday, when I was rereading *Les Cenci*, that I noticed a mistake previously unremarked, and was reminded of a long and tragic tale that begins at the family seat of the Corbera family in Sicily and ends at that of the Massimo family in Rome. The mistake occurs when we are told that the Pope, having been disposed to show mercy to Beatrice and the other prisoners, changed his mind and ordered the execution of the sentence upon hearing that Paolo di Santacroce had murdered his mother and recalling "also the fratricide committed by the Massimo brothers some time earlier."

But the woman killed by the two sons of Lelio Massimo was their stepmother, the young and beautiful

Euphrosyne of Syracuse; their crime was therefore not fratricide but something akin to matricide, though whether their motive was self-interested or honorable is not known. The Sicilian chronicler to whom we are indebted for the story of Euphrosyne seems inclined to regard her murder as an affair of honor, since he refers to the two assassins as "most honorable gentlemen" spurred on by grief and family disgrace. And, considering Euphrosyne's past, they had ample grounds for this.

Her name implied Joy, for among the three Graces Euphrosyne was the bestower of joy; and Linnaeus gave the name to a honey-colored butterfly prettily streaked with black. But this woman, familiarly known as Frosina, who was certainly young and beautiful and very probably foolish and cruel, neither gave nor received much joy in her short life; on the contrary, she proved to be, both for herself and others, a veritable harbinger of death.

Stendhal would have enjoyed the story to which, without realizing it, he had come so close, even though the greater part of it unfolded not in papal Rome but in viceregal Sicily. And the story actually begins with one of the viceroys, Marcantonio Colonna. Colonna conceived a passion for Euphrosyne, the wife of Calcerano Corbera, heir to the domains of Misilindino (which, following Philip II's decree *licentia populandi*, were about to become the site of the town later known as Santa Margherita Belice: and who can fail to remember that house built about a century later by one of the Filangeri family—and destroyed by earthquake four years ago—which plays a role of such mysterious grandeur in Lampedusa's *The Leopard*?). Having conceived this passion, he proceeded to lavish attention upon its object, to shower her with gifts and entertainments, justifying the epithet of "old fool" which his wife was wont to apply to him on such occasions.

"Lord Marcantonio," writes our Sicilian chronicler, "was so blinded by his passion that, careless of viceregal authority and reputation, he became a second Antony to his Cleopatra. He would follow or walk before her through the streets and even into church. Unmindful of all else, he frequented her constantly, by day with looks and compliments, by night with dutiful attentions. Many times was the viceroy seen alone and in disguise, making his way to her house by night . . ." Euphrosyne's husband, very young and perhaps none too intelligent, noticed nothing; but the affair was the talk of the whole city. And so it came to the ears of Don Antonio Corbera at Misilindino, where he was engaged in the founding of a town, and he decided to pay a visit to Palermo to see how things stood and set them right.

As soon as she heard of her father-in-law's decision, Euphrosyne "informed the Lord Marcantonio that she was in great danger, and that she had a greater fear of her father-in-law than of her husband." Colonna lost no time in thinking up a means of setting her free. Marcantonio's attitude towards the arresting of his subjects was generally

uninhibited, to say the least, but when it came to arresting Don Antonio Corbera he had a problem, for Don
Antonio had family connections within the Inquisition
and was therefore immune to arrest and trial by the
civil power and could only be brought before an inquisitorial court whatever the offense of which he was accused. This did not deter the viceroy. A bitter enemy of
the Inquisition and its officers, he nevertheless stooped
to ask a favor of the Inquisitor who was at that time Diego
de Haedo, a Benedictine and the author of a History of
Algiers that is an invaluable source of information about
the life of Cervantes. The Inquisitor fell for it—or perhaps
he was expecting a reciprocal favor which never materi-
alized, for in August 1581 we find him writing a letter of
complaint about it to the king consisting entirely of a
venomous indictment against Colonna.

Last year, Haedo writes, Marcantonio (whom he refers
to throughout by his Christian name only, with derision
and contempt) deceived us: he asked us, through Pompeo
Colonna, to suspend the Baron of Misilindino's privilege
as kinsman of the Inquisition, promising that a full explanation of the reasons behind the request would be
given later. But no sooner had we consented to the sus-
pension than he had him arrested for debt, though "the
entire populace is aware of his private motives for this."
It may seem strange that the Inquisitor fails to elaborate
on these "private motives," which were, of course, his relations with Euphrosyne, but to hint at the possibility of

some other motive was, in effect, more damaging to the viceroy than to specify an amorous involvement. In any case, Baron Antonio Corbera died in prison a few days after his arrest; some suspected poison, but the Inquisitor only refers to his sufferings.

There was still the husband to contend with, who, for all his naïveté, might eventually, however tenuously, put two and two together regarding the arrest and death of his father. The solution was to send him on a mission, led by Pompeo Colonna, to Malta, where another member of the expedition, one Flaminio of Naples, was apparently under instructions to do away with Corbera as soon as they arrived. We read: "Baron Calcerano Corbera was found one night dead of a great many stab-wounds behind the door of the house in which he was lodging, though he had excited neither the aversion nor the enmity of any man." He was twenty-one. And how old, one wonders, was Euphrosyne, now all alone and quite free.

But the victor of the Battle of Lepanto, now forty-nine, was neither alone nor free, and his wife, Felice Orsini, wise and indulgent woman though she was, was quite capable of putting the occasional spoke in his wheel. One night, in their palace, she knocked at the door of her husband's apartments, knowing full well that Euphrosyne was with him. In a panic, Marcantonio thrust the girl out onto the balcony with her clothes and instructions to get dressed; but he forgot about her sandals. Donna Felice swept into the room, announcing that she had come to sleep with her husband as the night was so bitterly cold, then, catching sight of the sandals, she exclaimed: "Now I see what a loving husband you really are. Have you bought those sandals especially for me?" And when her husband said he had, she laughed: "Ah, you old fool! Have you no more sense than to allow the poor girl to catch her death of cold out on the balcony?" And opening the balcony door, she hauled in the embarrassed and frightened Euphrosyne, comforted her and sent for a servant to accompany her home.

Marcantonio had a much more dangerous adversary, and one much more likely to poison (a word we should, perhaps, take literally) his pleasure in the almost untrammeled enjoyment of his lady-love, in the watchful Diego de Haedo. Of all the insults and injuries that the viceroy had directed at the Inquisition, none had bitten deeper than the stinging remark he had made to Haedo the last time they met: "The king can count my peers on one finger, he can fill his ships with yours."

Summoned to Spain, probably to exculpate himself of the charges contained in Haedo's indictments (set out in Garufi's *Contributo alla storia dell'Inquisizione in Sicilia*), Marcantonio Colonna sailed from Palermo on 1 March 1584, having recommended his mistress to the care of his wife in emotional and paternal terms, as the chronicler tells us, and promising that on his return he would arrange a marriage for Euphrosyne "to a person with whom she may live an honest life."

Expediency maybe, but Donna Felice either believed him or pretended to and assured him that Euphrosyne would stay with her at the palace "until it pleases God to send you home again." But it did not please God to send him home at all. He died on the road to Madrid, at Medinaceli, probably poisoned. Many saw the hand of the Inquisition in this, others that of the Spanish court, but no one seems to have given any consideration to Euphrosyne. She herself would not have been involved, of course, but someone who loved her might have been. So here's a little problem for historians with a taste for researching ancient documents: Was Lelio Massimo among those who accompanied Colonna on his journey to Madrid? He had certainly been very close to him during the years in Palermo and our chronicler records that he witnessed the very first skirmish with Euphrosyne, the games, the gallantry, the billing and cooing.

Could he not have been, even then, secretly in love with the woman, and is it not possible, in that case, that the affair between the woman he loved and his own powerful friend, which he was constrained to aid and abet, was causing him agonies of jealousy at every turn? If that is so, what is more likely—if indeed he were in the party—than that he should, blinded by passion and knowing himself to be above suspicion, and taking advantage of the disfavor into which Colonna was said to have fallen with the king, have yielded to the temptation of getting him out of the way? The passions are fierce task-masters, and they were fiercer still in the six-teenth century.

Of his love for Euphrosyne, however, there is no doubt, nor of the fact that he loved her beyond any sense of honor or of shame. Euphrosyne's name must have been notori-ous from Rome to Palermo for her part in the tragedy of the Corbera family (to the extent that her sisters-in-law had publicly, by means of a legal document, refused to ac-cept the return of any jewelry that she had worn) and for her flagrant adultery with the viceroy. But Lelio Massimo married her—having asked Donna Felice for her hand—and installed her in his own home. And it was to this house that the two "honorable gentlemen," Lelio's sons, came one day when their father was absent and, to put an end to their family shame and, possibly, public ridicule, "slew her with two light harquebuses." They were sub-sequently beheaded by the public executioner.

Our chronicler concludes: "Here is a most grave mat-ter with which to furnish a most pathetic tragedy." Pathetic indeed, and all very regrettable. But Stendhal, in his *Chroniques italiennes*, would have seen it in a very different light.

AUTHOR'S NOTE

THESE SHORT STORIES were written—together with a few more that seemed to me not worth collecting and reissuing—between 1959 and 1972. I have sought to put them in the order in which they were written (though not necessarily in the order in which they appeared in newspapers, magazines and anthologies), and I believe that the reader will be able to check the accuracy of the chronology by a comparison with the books that I published over the same period. Some are dated internally: "Demotion," for example, was written when Stalin's body was removed from the mausoleum (or rather, when the world was informed about it), and "Philology" when the anti-Mafia commission was set up (easy enough to foretell).

Of all the stories, only one has been revised and

substantially rewritten, that about Giufà and the cardinal. In the others, only the occasional oversight has been corrected.

My readers, with whom I believe I now have an excellent *rapport*, will certainly not question my decision to reissue the tales, since it was from them that the request initially came in the following fashion: when "A Matter of Conscience" was made into a feature film and two others, namely "End-Game" and "The Long Crossing," were televised, many requests were received from booksellers for those titles—which were unavailable, since the only form in which they had appeared was a slim volume entitled *Racconti Siciliani*, of which 150 copies, containing five stories and enhanced by an etching by Emilio Greco, had appeared under the impress of the Istituto Statale d'Arte di Urbino. But if the reader takes the matter for granted and is not disposed to ask for an explanation from me, I can still ask myself why I wanted to collect and reissue these stories. And my answer is that they seem to form, collectively, a kind of summary of my work up to now, from which one may see (and I cannot conceal from myself a certain satisfaction, within a context of more general and unceasing dissatisfaction) that during these years I have continued on my way, looking neither to the right nor to the left (and therefore looking both to the right and to the left), with no hesitation, no doubts and no period of crisis (and therefore with much hesitation, many doubts and periods of profound crisis); and that between the first and the last there is a certain feeling of having come full circle—not the same full circle as that described by a puppy chasing its own tail.

—L . S .

A B O U T   T H E   T Y P E

The text of this book has been set in Trump Mediaeval. Designed by Georg Trump for the Weber foundry in the late 1950s, this typeface is a modern rethinking of the Garalde Oldstyle types (often associated with Claude Garamond) that have long been popular with printers and book designers.

Trump Mediaeval is a trademark of
Linotype-Hell AG and/or its subsidiaries

Printed and bound by R. R. Donnelley & Sons,
Harrisonburg, Virginia

TITLES IN SERIES

HINDOO HOLIDAY
MY DOG TULIP
MY FATHER AND MYSELF
WE THINK THE WORLD OF YOU
J. R. Ackerley

THE LIVING THOUGHTS OF KIERKEGAARD
W. H. Auden, editor

SEVEN MEN
Max Beerbohm

PRISON MEMOIRS OF AN ANARCHIST
Alexander Berkman

A MONTH IN THE COUNTRY
J. L. Carr

HERSELF SURPRISED (First Trilogy, Volume 1)
TO BE A PILGRIM (First Trilogy, Volume 2)
THE HORSE'S MOUTH (First Trilogy, Volume 3)
Joyce Cary

PEASANTS AND OTHER STORIES
Anton Chekhov

THE PURE AND THE IMPURE
Colette

THE WINNERS
Julio Cortázar

MEMOIRS
Lorenzo Da Ponte

A HIGH WIND IN JAMAICA
THE FOX IN THE ATTIC (The Human Predicament, Volume 1)
THE WOODEN SHEPHERDESS (The Human Predicament, Volume 2)
Richard Hughes

THE OTHER HOUSE
Henry James

THE GLASS BEES
Ernst Jünger

THE WASTE BOOKS
Georg Christoph Lichtenberg